VOYAGE TO
YAHWEH

VOYAGE TO
YAHWEH

TAMISHA ROOSSIEN

PALMETTO
PUBLISHING
Charleston, SC
www.PalmettoPublishing.com

Copyright © 2024 by Tamisha Roossien

Paperback ISBN: 979-8-8229-3911-0

To *them*
Those that face real and raw torment of the mind.
Those that are given simple responses from others that simply
place a Band-Aid on a wound they are unequipped to look at.
Those that need a raw and real look at what it means to seek
Jesus even from their bed of darkness—without judgment.
May you find it here.

To *you*
All of you who have stood by me and dealt with my own
torment.
Who have sat with me through my struggles and led me to
Jesus, as I am attempting to do for others with this book.
I would not be here without you all.
You know who you are, and I love you all so very deeply.

TABLE OF CONTENTS

Ascending the Peak ·9

Handling the Truth ·24

Obeying the Crooks· ·41

Reuniting the Family· ·60

Meeting the Mr. and Mrs. ·77

Inviting the Lord ·93

Initiating the Intentions ·109

Daring the Board ·124

Praying the Prayers· ·139

Restoring the Dead ·151

ASCENDING THE PEAK

Silence encompassed the space between Joe and the magnificent though quite frigid terrain he now inhabited. It seemed even when the incandescent white powder fell from branch to branch with aid from a passing breeze, no sound was emitted. If it were not for his own two eyes seeing the transfer of snow, it would be as if the shift of nature had never occurred. An absolutely precise metaphor alluding to the reasoning behind this climb: to be alone, to seek out his identity. To release himself from his torment. Was there more to this world than what could merely be seen?

As the sting of the air pecked his cheek like a kiss from a cold lover, he became abruptly, overly aware of his existence—this was not a playful daydream, nor his imagination running wild yet again. His quest for sanity was as full of reality as one could experience. Not another deafening failure ringing through his bones, echoing through the rumors of his so-called earthly bloodline. A sigh of release: *peace, identity, sober mindedness.* The reminder of what he set out to discover chanted in his thoughts, breaking his trance.

Baker's Peak still towered above his six-foot frame; dark would be setting in soon, and seeking the night's campsite was now his primary focus. Joash, "the fire of God": what a hefty name to carry. It was doubtful that the warm hues flickering before him from his man-made fire embodied a mere fragment of an ember touched by God. Nor did he, as a man, even hold a portion of a flame to the small blaze burning the few twigs tossed in. Yet he bore the name of the highest fire in existence. He knew who "those Christians" said God was, who Jesus was supposed to be, and he had no desire to, or belief that he could, hold a candle to the actual fire of this God. The one that brought bitter laughter from his attitude at the thought of believing. This mindset was why he insisted all those he met call him simply Joe. Keeping up with the average Joe was a feat he was capable of conquering on most days or at least a goal he could brush with the tips of his fingers.

His fingers—not worn but soft. All due to lack of experience. Weak, with no hunger for personal growth unless it invited satisfaction and fulfillment of his lustful desires. He was covered in stains of soul-sucking pride that had crept further up his flesh with each finger point directing whoever stood cowering before him to manage his duties. All because of a name. Not the name one would assume might pour fear into the souls that crossed his path, "fire of God." Rather, it was the name that he carried, begrudgingly, from those he called family. The Lar name packed power throughout the nation. The historical figures that had borne it—the power was due to them. But for him, the name was false. A badge he had done nothing to earn yet seemingly could never be rid of. One that people forced to be his truth regardless of how obvious a lie it was. Tucked in his sleeping bag aside burning flames, he turned his focus back to April 13, 2014, at 3:12 p.m. The moment a veil deluded with false self-righteousness and false identity was torn away. Instantaneously replaced with hatred and paralyzing confusion.

The steel border of his desk, his seat for now, echoed with vibrations of tension as it received the taps of his anxious habit. One finger after the other landed on the icy surface in tense repetition. The roll of his head, cracking each vertebra, pounded in his eardrums. He had just argued his father into oblivion in their obnoxiously revisited dispute: "Joe, it's time you found an ounce of responsibility and stepped into the man you are due to become" and "No, *Father*, it's time you realize I am not capable of taking on full responsibility, as I have no desire to have my schedule ruled by responding to the people I can walk all over now."

A woman's voice tumbled through the halls, billowing in under the door of his office, disturbing his brooding. "Get him out of my sight! He is a scheming liar; this is utter nonsense." His mother's voice was warm at times, but in these moments, it was that of a heartless queen. "Off with their heads," Joe mumbled to himself, coupled with an empty chuckle. He strode over to the towering double doors of his office, sliding them apart enough to place himself in hearing range of the entire ordeal.

"Yes, ma'am, sir, I apologize, but you must leave now." Words almost whispered by an exhausted and severely apologetic door attendant. Depleted footsteps of a weary man marched slowly toward the exit. The noise of the flashback paired with the lingering crackle of coals woke Joe from the trip down memory lane. Vision blurred its way into existence. Snowflakes, following their guided paths, landing in their destined spot upon the earth. Or were they simply drifting with no designated purpose? The contemplation lasted mere seconds until his logical survival processing assumed its place in the lead, kindling the fire needed to fuel the continuation of his hike. Not only was he laying the foundation of twigs, conducting the process of swiping the match and lighting a physical flame, but he was, by sheer desperation, opening his mind, soul, and spirit to the possibility of a new foundation to be laid within. Though confusion, anger, hatred, fear, and doubt, along with a slightly desperate hope, simultaneously flooded his gut, he mustered the strength to force out the challenge to this God he had been challenged to investigate.

"If you exist, I need to know it. Show me. No games." Silence. His health did not match his youth. Though the number of years he carried made him far from old, his prime had passed. Most men his age were hitting the height of their physical abilities, while his health had peaked in college. The well-being of both soul and body. Acknowledgment of his weakness loomed over him, leaving him hungry for change, while his pool of willpower to pursue change was desolate and barren. His goals would continue to starve. Outwardly he looked like the average gym rat, but he was only a shell, deteriorating from the inside out. Partial destruction of his liver and Lord knows what else disguised as entertainment through his adolescence, followed by neglect from a three-year inebriated hibernation, had scoured him head to toe, soul, spirit, forcing nearly all signs of life to ooze from each pore to the uttermost infinitesimal drop. After approximately twenty minutes of walking, his breath became short.

A tremble waved through his flesh, prior to stiffness, causing his muscles to seize. Oxygen eluded his lungs for an instant as snow encompassed his knees, ending his collapse. Within his moment of exhaustion, he returned to the memory. Trauma was funny that way—memories make their way back in during your weakest moments.

"Mrs. Lar, ma'am…before my departure, I must encourage you to tell my son who it was that truthfully brought him into this world and who named him. We are all abundantly aware that you and your husband would never be capable of choosing a title for *your child* that invited the presence of God. In addition, be sure to advise that the document you allowed him to mindlessly autograph has now placed his entire family in more danger than simply being homeless. I am sure he would be interested in hearing that tale as well. If he has even a fragment of our heart, he may just have the sense to turn your decisions upside down and uncover the venom you direct to surge through this universe, to end its path of poisonous deceit and murder.

"Good day, Mary Ann…excuse me, Mrs. Lar."

The memory began to grow into a hallucination. Steady, on his knees, on the side of a mountain, he felt the familiar turmoil that arose within as he had eavesdropped in that doorway, as the gruff voice had rung in his ears and wormed its way across his flesh, creating an allure of the same ricketiness vibrating in his kneecaps as he walked toward his "mother" that day. Repulsed by the extent his flashbacks had reached, he paused, knowing he could not continue to ignore the memories. He had to face them to let them go. The battle had begun, and as labor goes, there was no stopping or turning back; no longer rooted on the sidelines, he hurled his emotions into the front lines, prepared to endure wounds from arrows of plagues his life had received by his own hand, the hand of others, the hand of the world, the hand of the enemy.

"I can't hear you!" His voice traveled through the rocks that formed the mass on which he was stationed. "I hear these fears! I hear the source of my anger! I hear every part of my humanity mocking me! But I cannot hear you, 'God.' Why can I not hear you? God! Reality, or what mankind has manufactured into reality, shows me you do not even exist."

Halting in his words, turning his face to the sky, the pure white Heaven above him, directing his attention to the pulsing heart that dwelled privately within his chest cavity, he went on, "Yet here I am! Here I am, having no ability to sincerely understand whom it is I am speaking to, asking you to answer me. Hoping that I will want you, hoping that I will love you, hoping that within seeking you, I will no longer be worthless, that I will transform from the waste of the world into a partially decent man! I demand you let me hear you. Otherwise, why couldn't you have just left me at my desk in the dark? You could have not called my father to come to find me. This is why all that happened, right? Because you wanted me to find you? Wanted me to invite you into my life? Right? That is why I am here, right? Because you called me, right? Right!"

Faint impressions rose from his core to the surface of his cheeks, resulting in flushed skin. Neither a still, small voice nor one loud and booming came as a response to his groaning. Rather, a hush fell upon him. He became immediately enthralled with the lull he was suddenly bathed in. Beyond what the altitude was able to filch, this ejected all breath he possessed. Peace. Complete peace beyond any other. Was this what they meant by *Prince of Peace*? Excitement dwindled—or was it a natural calmness derived from spiked serotonin from releasing this torture through his vocal cords? Debate performed a dominating waltz in his brain, yet he basked in his moment of unorthodox serenity. Next, a surge of delight filled his spirit to the brim and poured over. Bringing himself back into his true existence, he shook his head. As he glanced around, he saw a blanket of powder, the slate rocks emerging among the arctic covering. "God, is this you?" Boyishly, the words squeaked from his lips. Never such a vulnerability had he met.

Vulnerability in a man was a *sin* according to those in his world; it was a place he was previously never willing to visit. A question exceedingly elementary yet settling in his core, he had an honest expectancy of a response. "Does God actually exist?" By no means an audible sound. No, an utterance entirely mute arising out of the crux of his spirit. *A still, small voice.* Any logical man would try to state that Joe hearing anything was "nonsense, merely your own mind. Your mind is far greater a power than you claim, my friend. Any morsel of bliss encountered, any voice you hear, is solely your mind choosing happiness over turmoil. Or insanity." Never before had he felt less of an urge to dispute that carnal lecture of rationale. Not one microscopic point was there in paying any mind to that argument; he was entirely incapable of proving the absolute Truth he had just caught a glimpse of to anyone, even to his version of Mr. Hyde, desperate to substantiate the lack of a supreme being as the Creator.

Standing from his knelt-down position, Joe noticed a sense of belief, a fresh understanding formulating in his heart, as though wisdom were being placed upon him. Maybe insanity was not what drove those who sought and followed Jesus. Though this awakening was breathtaking, Joe was far from unaware of the lengthy voyage ahead of him. Beyond conquering this peak, he would need to invest his years in the pursuit of Heaven and the one who occupied it. That is, if he did not leave the mountain back in the mindset of denying His existence, if God was real and more than real, enough. Time would tell. All he had was time—time and solitude. Progressing along in the expedition, appearances of the heart's painful souvenir hissed by in sore remembrance. A flinch initially in response but swiftly soothed as though by a firm yet tender hand atop his shoulder, granting comfort. A hunger to face the recollection in pursuit of healing, no more an infuriating vexation jabbing to escape from his subconscious. His steps were not halting for an instant; his mind was making way for an approach fervent for pure transformation as opposed to an outlook hell-bent on saturating all he knew with vengeful anger. Joe began to deliberately search for the past responsible for the pain he was looking to have removed from his spirit. He began to sketch the memory with control.

Lines penciled in windows and walls, charcoal smudged in the dusky floors—all the while, his agitated pulse broke the silence. Along the side of a mountain, his mouth took on the dryness, and the lump returned to his throat, so familiar as a choking mass. "Hold it! Mother, who is this? Why am I hearing him speak of me as his son? And how does he know you as Mary Ann? I thought you had kept that name a secret from all but our immediate family."

Thickened hush swelled, overflowing every last nook. Eardrums would be blown by hair falling to the floor. A newly sharpened blade would have been unable to leave a mark on the tension. "Joash...I...Joe." The transfer between names was initiated by a twitch from Joe in revolted response to the first title she uttered.

"You were not due to be home for days. Never you mind; this man is psychotic and is being removed from our presence. Nothing you need to fret about. Go rest. Your travels to our investors was lengthy and exhausting I'm certain."

His mother's quick attempt to hush the issue was ignored. "Quiet. I am not naive; do not patronize me. I want to hear it from him."

His eyes leaped and bore into the core of the man timid before him. A second glance did not come close to being passed in the direction of the woman he was rapidly losing trust in, for reasons he could not begin to comprehend. The stranger, bearing the scent of coolant, street, and Cohiba Robusto freshly puffed, shifted his posture when his eyes met Joe's. Fear released its grip on the man when he was not gazing into the face of Joe's mother. In its place came a firm stance. In a moment he embodied coarse strength, wisdom any youthful child would envy, and sorrow elders would hold a ceremony to honor. Yet he spoke not, a silent, steady oak.

"Sir, follow me, please." The pleasantry escaped Joe's lips before he had a chance to blink. When had the last sentence involving any form of nicety escaped his lips? Their steps coincided along the path back beyond the doors in which Joe's earth had begun to shatter. He could feel his mother's stare following them; he could sense her eyes slowly shift to the floor as they entered his office.

She knew better than to stop this. Though he respected the woman who'd raised him, from whence his course was decided, she had no power to change his map in the slightest. "I hope that this office being distanced from the woman who so clearly intimidates you will release your tongue. As you can imagine, my mind is frantically searching for answers to questions formed regarding your monologue performed moments ago, and you will not be free to leave until those questions are fulfilled entirely to my desire."

The words drifted through the room as he took his place behind the desk. Never would he speak of how small he felt as he peered toward the man before him. "Sit, please."

Taking a seat, the man finally uttered his first words to Joe. "Centuries have come to pass since I watched your brow furrow. It does tend to pack far more power now than the innocence it carried all those years ago as I witnessed our friends place you in your mother's arms..." Before Joe could protest in dissatisfaction, the man continued. "I must request that you grant me your patience as I muster the capability to share with you such precious though dangerous truths. In 1982, I had begun preparing for my transition of duties as the upcoming COO of Reis Corporations. Towering, my father's company led the nation in the news with their paper. Not typically a man driven by social status, my father chose to host an unexpected introduction ceremony announcing and formally initiating my new title. Posted in a corner, hidden at my own party, holding the same Macallan pour served to my palm hours ago, I watched. I watched as a room full of boys called men competed with their erroneous stories, none truly believable to a sober ear but eaten up by every lightweight in sight. I watched as girls called women labored, often ineffectually, to steal the attention of the savage competitors. When one prevailed in her conquest, a poor lad chaotically pursued the lass, only to be dismissed as if he had displayed an absurd audacity in his attempt."

He paused; Joe saw a sickness seem to permeate the man from head to toe. He stood pouring water from his pitcher. "Drink. Take a moment to collect yourself," Joe demanded.

Nodding, the man reached for the glass. One gulp as if having just escaped a drought, a dejected sigh, and he continued. "An enchantress she was. From head to toe, declaring that she was of the same class as those bustling around her carrying an ambiance of fortune. Yet her eyes bore such an unpretentious... warmth. My stride began without my consent in quest of her post. That night I fell. Anyone—including me, then—would have deemed it love. Yet in the coming weeks spent between my family and hers as they planned our nuptials, concealed malevolence emerged. I recall a supper within her home. A third instance of the bride and her folks removing themselves for a private discussion had occurred. An inquiring mind thought it best to ensure I was able to overhear my bride's intimate session. It was amid such an undercover operation that I understood who my bride, Mary Ann Peleske, truly was. The Peleskes were loyal to the corruption boss himself, Joey Sombrano."

Joe flinched at the name. Though Sombrano was no longer in their midst, having been overrun years ago by two less-than-dishonorable henchmen who themselves had met an early grave due to such brainless bravery, the crime lord's name still brought with it a chill of the spine. "My assumption, per your activated expression, is that you understand the power the Peleskes held by even being in the same circle as Big Joe, let alone being his closest company. Mary Ann's innocence, shown through her gaze that night, was indeed a brilliant façade well practiced and used to hypnotize even the most discerning of men.

"Had I not risked my dignity by eavesdropping that night, I would have been another casualty, my heart her trophy of the kill. From their discussion, I learned their sight had been fixed on my father's paper for a long time. Our marriage was their advantage to arrogate a growing business from the inside. So as not to alert the public of their fiendish manners, they would claim that my father graciously chose to share his obtained wealth with his in-laws while indeed the Peleskes would own everything my father created."

A lone crystal landing on Joe's lashes stirred him out of his remembrance yet again. He sensed the need to center his attention on the growing anger in his heart toward the Peleske family. He carried such a loathing for them all. An opportunity to forgive his enemies was never desired prior but now seemed to be a primary goal; if such a path would help him heal, he would seek it.

A pardon fueled by pure mercy out of his soul and off his lips to be poured out upon a people entirely unworthy. There was no want to forgive. His heart, a complete stone, longed not to let go but instead to obtain revenge. "Give me justice! You can see the anger burning my core, God. Strike them! I long to see your hand come down on them, to annihilate their complete existence!"

Instantaneous sorrow gripped him fully. A voice from within spoke in a whisper. "You are not worthy either, yet I provide you new mercies each morning." The conviction appeared as if from directly beside him and within the innermost bowels of his quintessence in the same. Tears stained his frozen flesh, and his arms rose gradually above his head.

"Thank you, God! I heard you! I heard Him! I heard the voice of God!" Echoes pranced about; no care arose if others inhabited the mountain near him.

The joy of hearing the voice he had set out in hopes of experiencing was far too great to contain. "I suppose I forgive them, God. Yet as I say that my heart still holds a large bit of contempt for them. I long to, with your help, release them fully."

It is undoubtedly awe-inspiring what the voice of Yahweh can inflict upon one's spirit. This was working. Joe had set out to find God, to heal, forgive, to release, and it was working. Once again, he willingly dived into a darkened past with new faith to further this supernatural healing. Again, the voice of George filled Joe's memory.

"The rest of the evening I feigned ignorance, doting on Mary Ann and seeking the approval of her parents as any oblivious suitor would. When I arrived home with my folks, dread rolled in. I vomited the truth. Mom's and Dad's eyes revealed knowledge that our lives were those of puppets forevermore.

"The Peleskes owned us. Yet my parents' love, their unyielding love and their pride, allowed them not to submit. My father met with Mr. Peleske one evening, and after that, we went into hiding. Staying in New York, we moved to the gutter. All we had was robbed of us. It was not until the year 1990, after I had met and fallen in love with my wife Donna and we had conceived our son, that my dad made me aware of the topic of discussion between him and that snake of a man. Dad had gone to negotiate our release and left having turned his paper over to the crook Peleske. The paper kept the same name so as to not disturb society, but all ownership was stripped from my father in place of our freedom. Though we could never truly claim liberty. We would forever be the bug under their microscope. One misstep and they would have us killed.

"I was informed simply because I requested my father allow us to move back to proper civilization to raise our child, only to realize that luxury would never be available to us again. July fourteenth of 1991, our boy arrived. Though our belongings were diminutive, he brought Donna and me all we would ever need.

"Three days, not even the full seventy-two hours. The length of time we had our son. On July seventeenth, around ten at night, a pounding on the metal sheet of our rigged door woke us. I rushed to open it, assuming an emergent matter was at hand with it being so late. Upon my invitation, two men entered the shelter, a third directly behind the larger couple emerging from between his security and a fourth, Mr. Peleske himself. The stranger led me to an empty area in the home, if you could call it that. An abandoned hotel. His minions removed from their coats two glasses, along with scotch. Pouring both of us a bit and serving us silently, Peleske stood still behind him. We studied one another until finally, he spoke.

"*Gideon Lar, husband of Marie Lar, formerly known as Mary Ann Peleske.* He shared with me a truth about him and his wife. That their family was due to be an utter disgrace, as she was barren. Of course, they had to save their lineage and carry forth the Lar name. Son, Joash, my boy, they claimed you as their own that night. They had been observing us the entire term of the pregnancy. Once it was confirmed that a boy was born, they made their move. I fought…I fought with every bit of fury I could muster, but they struck your mother and me both within an inch of our lives…I could not…" The man's eyes rose to meet those of Joe, who was now filled with more rage at once than any other man could ever have claimed. "I am your father, Joash. George Reis."

HANDLING THE TRUTH

The darkness that lowered itself upon that room, deep enough to cause midnight to appear vibrantly pale, drenched the two men as they fell mute. His eyelids closing, alertness involuntarily disabled Josh's body, now responding to a statement he had to strive to grasp. As he drew in a deep breath, the air tasted sour. No flash of life, no montage of days spent with Mr. and Mrs. Lar, zoomed across his vision. He was just stunned by emptiness at first, then found his thoughts adrift amid a vast, raging sea. Tossed and turned. Perplexity encompassed any ideas that floated through his mind. A vessel of timber, the painted word "Life" plastered along its side, increasingly mangled from emotional waves ripping at its seams. Knocking shattered the quiet. Standing to his feet, Joe stumbled his way, only semiconscious, to the door. Upon opening it and staring into Marie's eyes, he woke fully.

"Enter, *Mother*. Take a seat. But do not speak until I am finished."

The woman made her way through the room with false arrogance, only given away by the slight trembling triggered by fear of her son's sudden realization of her deafening deceit.

Removing himself from the recollection and taking a seat in the snow, Joe rifled through his pack for food. Pausing, turning his gaze toward the long path behind him, which revealed his fresh trekking, he took in all he had faced thus far. Diving into the pain of his path for healing, diving into the faith of his future to know Jesus. Already there had been treacherous hills and valleys of emotion. Pain and joy playing tug-of-war, all the while searching for one main treasure, his identity. His false identity had been lost; if he had a true identity anywhere within, he needed to know it.

Longing grew—to remain soaked in this refining torture. Wisdom overflowed the rim of his skull, bringing with it awareness that this transformation was going to be worth all the pain endured. A chuckle escaped his chapped lips as he realized how weak his body was. The immeasurable strength to hike through both the reality of the winter he sat amid and the reality of the memories he placed focus on to devour—had it come solely from the God of the universe? *This level of strength to climb this mountain midwinter and mid–psychotic break could not be attained by any mere human.*

He rolled the thought over and over. To count it all "joy" was a term most had heard, including him, throughout this godless walk he was just now hoping to emerge from. Preposterous and impossible the quote was until now. Were all of his previous thought patterns going to be broken during the search for

God? Excitement, that of a little child, grew, as he imagined how much more transformation would come as he took his steps closer to Jesus. He reached for the hem of his garment on repeat.

Not once had the thought ever graced his being that finding God would be simple. He was a man of science. Beliefs that could be proven and physically seen were the only *truths* he would ever give a splinter of attention to. Hearing of those who claimed to believe in an all-powerful being existing everywhere, including a place such as Heaven, which was impossible to discover without death, never brought more out of him than contempt for such heinous ideals. Along with mockery of those who chose to live their life as though it were pure fact. Prayer escaped his lips in times of drunkenness that brought him close to an early grave, but never did he truly direct them to God himself. 'Twas merely an empty and pathetic attempt to stop the room from spinning and the stomach acid from rising. If only—if only someone had told him this, that all you needed do was ask with a puny sliver of faith and hope, and the God of all, Yahweh, Jehovah, He would respond. He would show. Who knows, maybe some devout follower of Christ had tried to guide Joe to see this opportunity, but he had shoved it aside with disdain. Sorrow, tasting of complete bitterness, consumed his drying mouth. Analytical questions about life, death, the world, God, and the universe swarmed through his mind countless times, forming questions to which answers were conceived in passive aggressive stances.

As in, if the response did not meet your exact understanding or simply did not make sense to you, it was void and worthy of dismissal and judgment. Of those questions and challenges, which of them did people already know and answer because they were aware of the existence of a Creator? Yet such beliefs were shoved under a rug because they hindered our wants and our desires. His plan would still unfold. His love would still be unwavering for His creation. That cross still bore the same gift. So why was there such anger over the deceit Marie had brought into his life and the lives of his parents? It did not change the fact that God existed, nor that He was omnipotent and Lord of all. Would God still not use Joe? His parents? Even his false parents? Would not the orchestra of His voice still not command His plan? Had not God allowed this path to be created by the enemy's hand, knowing how beautifully He could use it for His kingdom in the future? Was Joe not still safe in his Heavenly Father's hand regardless of the chaos ensuing around him?

Yet Joe could not shake the question: Could he have heard the voice of the one who knitted him within his mother's womb years prior? Would souls have been protected from the vile mistreatment he spewed due to the wretched man he had become, following in the Lars' footsteps? Had he been raised by his real parents in the first place...

These questions were visited time upon time throughout the years spent in his mental prison after finding out his identity was a lie. The walls he sank into, the bars he faded behind as he allowed the horror of the life he had been brought up in to consume him. "God, bitterness has lain stagnant within the confines of my soul as sewage rotting in an abandoned pipe. Rust formed over and imprisoned any emotion from me in response to the events unfolding before my eyes, making me bury my humanness instead. You have received pure refusal from me, your son, to even look in the direction of the pain coursing along my bones. Let alone begin to clean the disorder it has left in its wake.

"Not a single want to heal was within my wishes before these past days. Not one day before the decision to tackle this physical mountain had I the urge to face the truth of where I came from, the truth of who the people who raised me turned out to be. To open my eyes to the pit I sank into once I was made aware of this disgusting truth, the truth of the man I have lived as throughout my sorry existence. Yet you still sit patiently with open arms, awaiting my decision to embrace you, as if blind to my stubbornness."

Allowing his eyelids to fall, Joe turned his mind like a channel to the episode that aired directly following his awareness of the news. The look on Marie's face when she entered proved that he did not need to confirm with her the truth; her trembling spoke the truth with magnificent volume. As soon as her body language supplied the answer, guilt swept through Joe's bones.

"George, how can I reach you? Where are you staying?" Joash grabbed a pen and paper to record the address, not removing his glance from the two sitting before him.

"Joash, I know all of this has come to you as a severe shock, and rightfully so. It was never my intention to disrupt your life here, but I have a wife and I have a daughter, Emilee, your sister." Seeing the immediate rage that crossed Joe's face, George explained quickly and loudly, almost yelling, "No, Joe, your adopted sister. If you had a biological sister, I am sure we would have come to you sooner. We adopted Emilee when her mother passed of cancer, which was rather quick due to homelessness not providing the best health care coverage. We were her verbally confirmed godparents, as Linda, her mother, was the first to help us get acclimated to life on the street. She took care of us with what little belongings and grand knowledge she had. She even delivered you. So naturally, when she passed, her six-year-old daughter became our adopted child. That was in ninety-five. She is grown, beautiful, strong, and wise.

"She stays with us out of feeling responsible to pay us back for raising her; no matter how hard we try to encourage her to seek more for her life, she states that God's plan for her is with us for now. Who are we to argue with the Almighty? Son, we have this family, this community whom I feel entirely responsible for protecting. Somehow being abandoned to their neighborhood by the Peleskes and kept there by the Lars means that your mother and I are responsible for protecting them. The question is, would this area have even been on the Lars' radar to tear down for their gain and our destruction had it not been the 'home' we occupied?

"I knew when I saw the panic in the faces as one of our men came running down the block to our main gathering place, yelling for everyone's attention, panicking and shakily reporting that he heard the news in the city that this was to become the new version of SoHo, with 'homeless repellents' nonetheless, that I needed to do whatever it took to put an end to this attempt to destroy my family. The property you signed on to demolish for your new project has an entire village of homeless people occupying it, including your mother and me. That is where we can be found."

Joe had felt a strange rush of sorrow flood his chest.

The air grew thick enough that it was impossible to draw a breath. Lies unraveling around him chipped away at everything he was, almost as though his existence were entirely false, a dream someone had just woken him from. Acid crept up his throat, and his mind was in a complete fog. It was a disappearing act—he was fading from life. Panic struck, and Satan's lies began to seep in, smooth as truth.

You cannot allow your identity to be wiped from the face of the earth. You are the man you are; allow not one soul on this earth to change you, lest ye die. Do not sit idly by as control of your life and who you are slips through your fingers. The outcome of losing control is a prison; do not allow this man who showed up unexpectedly into your life to rip that control away from you. You have had every choice to leave the Lar home. You chose to be this man; no one made you this way. Do not let anyone steal your identity—being Joe Lar is your identity. You will become invisible; you will wither away. They will *have power over you, and they will abuse it.*

Joash was oblivious to the notion that the devil himself, the father of lies, was the whisper behind these thoughts provoking this hefty albeit calm anger to seethe from within. "My mother is right—Mr. Reis, you need to leave."

One last drop of hope sprang to life within the broken father's eyes, immediately fading away like dust in the wind.

"I see…" The whisper barely tumbled off his lips as he stood, completely still, with no emotion on his face. "Son, though I cannot say I feel faith within me right now, I still choose faith. I still trust in my God that He will open your eyes to the truth. Whether it be in time to save our home or not, that is His will. He remains God and Lord of my life regardless. You, also, will always remain my son, no matter the man you choose to be. But let me advise this: I suggest you take time to yourself to learn to no longer look down your nose with hatred but instead turn your eyes to your Father in Heaven with surrender. You need Him, and He is simply awaiting your realization of that truth. *Come to Me, all who are weary, and I will give you rest.* That is a call from Jesus on your life, son. I know your spirit is weary, whether you will admit it to yourself or not. Go to Him; I pray you will."

One final glance between father and son, both searching one another's face as if trying to unbury whatever lived beneath the surface, one final sigh escaping a father's lips, holding him back from speaking any further words and placing himself in the way of God's plan by ministering without guidance. Lastly, his departure.

George made each step strong, sturdy, calculated, calm but quick. Doing his best to remove himself with dignity even though he was crumbling on the inside. That was the last Joe had seen of his father. Having no more memory of the instance to recollect, Joe removed himself from the memory one last time. Roughly two thousand feet in elevation to go, by Joe's un-educated calculations. Time for one more night of camp before he would reach the peak.

Taking a brief gander, Joe searched for a safe base to set up for the evening. Turning and looking out over all the ground covered the past couple of days, he felt numb. His mind was exhausted. Finally, a laugh escaped his lips. The absolute insanity! Poor little Joe had had truth dropped on him about the lie he had grown up in, and it had led to this. It had led to years of tearing his body apart with alcohol and starvation. It had led to words spoken by a stranger who so happened to be his biological father about the possibility of "God" existing to gnaw at him for those drunken months. Enough to send him on an exhibition up a damn mountain in search of *his soul and the creator of it.* He must have simply been mad. Wait, but what of the voices, the supernatural peace, the responses to his calling out to "God"?

"What of it!" Joe grumbled. "This is pathetic."

This was a pathetic attempt to find help from the great Almighty because the alcohol was no longer numbing the pain. The pain he should not have even been feeling. So his family was filled with monsters and turned him into one right along with them. This world was eat or be eaten—why be such a wimp and whine about the hand life had dealt him? Collapsing and slamming his fist through the snow, into the ground, he did not stop until pain enveloped his knuckles and numbness eventually took over. Why couldn't he just make up his mind already? Was there a God or wasn't there? If so, was He loving and a helper or a hateful punisher? Was it God's voice he had heard, or was it his sensitive emotions attempting to force an answer? Why did his mind have to be a complete mass of twisted confusion? What was the point of forgiveness—why did he even have to get over this mess his life had become? It would be simple to shove it all aside, go back to work, and ignore the filth. He had learned how to be fake long ago. When he was fake, he got whatever he wanted. He had power and control.

He was blissfully spoiled rotten. It was easy. Easier than trying to face his pain, easier than forgiving himself and anyone else who had invited hell to enter his life. Easier than trying to believe in an invisible God and take that path less traveled to follow Him. Just easier. Back when his mind was merely logical and selfish, when a woman, a new car, ordering others around, or a night of complete recklessness would make all his troubles fade away—his troubles were far easier then, or maybe he simply cared less. As much as he longed to go back to that carefree state of living, the conviction that drenched him from George's goodbye speech would not allow him to let go of the notion of God. Yet if God existed, why had He been so silent about His existence up until now? Why could Joe look out at the world and seem to see no proof or even a hint that there was a Creator? After George left his office that day, Joe immediately found himself outside the same bar he frequented, filled with the same suits, the same slicked-back hair, and the same one glass of rich whiskey they would all sip on for hours.

He could not bring himself to step through that door, into that familiar falseness carried by those clowns. He sped off again and stopped slowly outside of a bar that screamed disease. That hole-in-the-wall was all he wanted to crawl into at that moment. That first night he simply had a couple of drinks and found his way back home in time to pass out. As his heart hardened over the ordeal, as the visions of the crimes the Lars had committed plagued his thoughts, his attendance at Trivi's Bar grew substantially in frequency.

His assistant had come in once and found Joe slumped in a corner, covered in his own vomit. Bill knelt to meet Joe's face; Joe managed to force out one command: "Leave." Bill scoffed, ripping his name tag off his suit and dropping it at Joe's feet; he stormed out and never returned. Joe battled between thoughts that he had every right to fall off the face of the earth into the world of substances and that he had no right at all to climb into such a deep hole of self-pity, harming not only himself but anyone within any close distance of him. The deeper he had dug into drunkenness, the louder the words about God had echoed in his ears.

He could not seem to escape the call to investigate the existence of God, no matter the number of times he worked tirelessly to drown the call in whatever liquor the bar owned. One evening, as he drowned off the side of the SS *Trivi*, a stranger entered. Joe's consistent appearances had allowed him time to familiarize himself with all the regulars; this guy was new.

Walking in looking ragged and defeated, he plopped himself next to Joe at the bar. "Scotch, no rocks." The man's voice was depleted of energy. His beard was somehow both thick and patchy, knotted, and dirty. His hands shook from severe Parkinson's, yet when he gripped the glass and lifted it to his lips, his fist was steady as a rock. "I know you." The man mustered a whisper in Joe's direction.

"Forget it, pal, I'm not up for a conversation with a crazy bum—not drunk enough yet." Joe spat.

"I ain't crazy, Joe, just familiar with the face that signed some defeated people's death sentence and all. George's boy, right?"

Joe's scowl turned into a look of distrust along with increased curiosity. "Ah, you're one of them...and you and George know one another?" Joe asked, stiffening his expression so as to appear in control, although the mention of those people seemed to sober him up with guilt immediately.

"Ha, well, I know George. George knows the same folks I know, but he does not know this version of me. I tend to stay hidden." Pausing and taking another sip, the man let out a sly smirk before he continued. "So, you figure it out for yourself yet?" the man asked, without even glancing in Joe's direction.

"Excuse me?" Joe raised an eyebrow in demand.

"Your identity. Have ya figured out your identity for yourself yet?"

The question furthered Joe's sobriety. "Listen, man, I do not know how my business is any concern of yours. I suggest you stop prying into the life of someone you have never even met." Joe stared at the man as he just sat staring straight ahead, not saying a word. Assuming the authority in his voice had scared the man enough to mind his own business, Joe scoffed and turned back to face forward, all the while an inquisition poking at his core. How had this man known any information if George did not know who he was? The rumor mill, maybe. One had to assume a small village of homeless people carried gossip faster than the speed of light since it most likely gave them a reason to live that day. Something juicy.

"George was correct in his instruction to you, son. You need God in your life, and this identity crisis is a call to find him. But you won't answer; I won't let you. Give up, and just kill your liver. I'll help. Next round is on me."

Joe's face flushed with anger, and he turned, planning to beat this man for the sheer audacity. But as Joe turned, the seat was empty, the glass gone. "Bartender! Hey, bartender!" Joe demanded.

"Calm it, Joe. You're going to cause panic. What the hell are you screamin' about?" Tobie snapped back.

"Where did the bum that was just sitting next to me go?" Joe asked.

"Bud, I know you ain't had that many yet. There ain't been another dude in here aside from you and Johnny over in his usual corner, so I suppose this bum is wherever he's been all morning, 'cause it ain't been in here." Tobie's response rang in Joe's ears for a moment. The man—who was that man? Joe had had an entire conversation with a man who had never entered the establishment. Yet was sitting right next to him. So close Joe could smell his filth. Joe stood to his feet as calmly as possible; while in a fog on the inside, he was coming apart at the seams.

He had been writhing with discomfort to rid his memory of the words George had spoken about God for months now, and suddenly a dingy bum had appeared, knowing of this recent crisis, and insisted that George was right and, what's more, that he was going to aid in Joe's death, keeping him from answering the call. How had he known the exact words George had used? This had to have been a manifestation of Joe's subconscious thoughts over time. That explanation brought a slight peace, as it seemed quite logical, yet Joe could not peel himself out of that bar quick enough. He needed to get out, go home, lie down, and sleep it off.

"Hey, Joe, man, ya still owe me for your drinks! Crazy fool." Tobie shook his head, watching Joe run out of his front doors.

Making it back to his apartment, he collapsed atop his mattress, not even removing his boots. As he rolled over, his eyes roamed the structure of his home. Another hole-in-the-wall he had begun renting immediately after the family secrets were uncovered. His "mother" Marie had found it at one point and made an appearance simply to state that she and Mr. Lar would allow him to wallow for as long as he needed but expected him back at the company for the next project, adding comments about her pride in his not having removed his signature from the demolition contract. As Joe lay there, he drifted into sleep. His dreams filled with the man from the bar. He woke with the voice of the man still audible, as if the man's face were present right before him, the stench still in Joe's nostrils. The same sensation clouded him: *death.*

Joe had a new sensation that he needed to rid himself of this torment that was creating hallucinations. He needed to be in solitude, away from the dark streets that called him to drink. He sat in front of his computer sipping three-day-old cold coffee and began typing: "Where to go to clear your head." The park, shopping, rehabs, church, books. Nothing called to him.

He tried again: "Where to go to get away." Vacation ideas, plane tickets, hotels, nothing but places with people. One more try: "Where to go to escape torment and find your identity."

Scrolling down the page of vague answers, he came across an article titled "Conquering a Mountain, Finding Myself." Joe read every word carefully, cold sweats coming and going, bringing with them the panic of seeing the man again, feeling as though he was clearly going insane. Part of him longed to see the stranger, as if his presence were proof of something beyond his human existence, terrifying yet inexplicable proof. Shaking his head, once he had finished reading, he had made his choice—Baker's Peak it would be. He would clear his head, get back in shape, and maybe leave with a sense of direction. In fact, he would even seek out God. Just to prove He did not exist. Rid himself of this nonsense. "Yeah, here I am on the side of a mountain, trying to clear my head and rid myself of insanity, all because a man who wasn't even real scared me into it."

Joe mocked himself. As he settled into his bag once again, his spirit was defeated, his logical answers were consuming any hope of there being a God. He felt foolish for believing he had heard him and frustrated that his mind was twisting further into debate and confusion. He would head down tomorrow, back to his safe seat in Trivi's. Regret and humiliation flooded his thoughts as he drifted off to sleep.

"Jeremiah 33:3." Joe woke to the words whispered directly into his ear and sprang up out of his bag, nearly falling over, grabbing his knife as quickly as his frozen fingers would allow. "Who's there! I have a weapon!" Joe threatened the darkness of the night. Nothing but silence arose in response to his shouts. Joe calmed, realizing it was *nothing but a realistic dream.* He sat and caught his breath. The words reclaimed a spot in his thoughts: "Jeremiah 33:3." He became aware in his grogginess that this was a Bible verse.

He had never cracked open a Bible nor spent any significant time with those who had. Although, since part of this journey was originally dedicated to the investigation of God, he had packed a small one. Staring at his pack with anxiousness, he reached in its direction, wiggling the small paper book from its assigned pocket. Turning it over in his hands, he hardly had time to think before he flipped through to the book in question, using his head lamp to guide him. Joe could not help but read the passage aloud. "Call to me, and I will answer you and will tell you great and hidden things that you have not known."

Joe had heard the term "God's word is alive" before. When one lived in New York, street preachers were frequent encounters. Yet now he could feel his spirit transforming with wisdom, as though gears were physically shifting within his chest. Grinding away doubt, slowly, with the grasping of God's reality taking its place. Joe's eyes were further opened to the Truth of the kingdom of Heaven being more real than the earth he experienced firsthand. Disbelief was diminishing.

Waking that final dawn, he began his descent, no longer in a state of defeat but instead setting out on a new passage. One to find George. One filled with a hunger to learn so much more about the devil that had met him in his pit within Trivi and the God that the Bible said was capable of defeating said enemy.

One with questions about knowing what voices were true and which were deceit. One that he seemed to now grasp would not be easy but would at least lead him to what he longed for most, pure Truth.

He had no more encounters on his way down; he had no real energy to ask for them just yet. He needed counsel first, from someone who knew far more about all of this than he. "Here's to some unexpected father-son time," Joe muttered, looking up to the heavens one last time as he drove away from the trailhead.

OBEYING THE CROOKS

He had finally faced his son and from that encounter, rejection. A sour quiver of questioning rose in his stomach. "Why, God, would you call me, your son, to step out in faith, obedient to you, reassuring me that you would save my family, only to allow my son to reject you and me both? What is your plan for this pain? How will you save us now if Joash has so resolutely refused my plea?"

Though anger, fear, and confusion whipped about, George knew his God was bigger than the rejection of one mere man. "Your will be done, Father. Forgive me for questioning you." Trusting the Lord despite all circumstances surrounding him was not a task that came easily to George; only his journey through the pits of hell within his lifetime was responsible for teaching him how to have faith in God when logic said there was no reason to. Often, George would rise early, prior to the rest of the city rising around him. He would roam the streets and buildings searching for food, coming up empty, only lessening his faith and growing his anger toward God.

Seemingly endless structures mocked him, their bones groaning, announcing their age, reminding him of his rocky foundation. Though brilliant light beamed through blue skies, though warmth was carried in the air, there seemed to be a gray border surrounding the slums George resided within. A permanent chill raked his spine daily. Each body that roamed through the abandoned businesses carried its own storm composed of blackened skies and freezing downpours, their souls writhing within them, begging to be taken. The sun did not shine here. Guilt clamped his heart the moment he returned from his meeting with Joash, and he noticed the sound of his own daughters' laughter triggered nothing from his numbness any longer. That was the match that struck the gasoline fueling his subdued anger. The wind pushing against his flesh, his bones nearly failing his attempt to sprint as far away as possible from those around him so as to not startle them with the outburst boiling beneath his calloused surface; his bloody feet, rubbed raw from sockless shoes, carried him to the edge of the roof on the farthest building away from any family members who would talk him down.

Why was he still breathing? Why did any of them exist? Satan began to whisper his lies; either God had created them as a joke or there was no God. All his life George had experienced the peace of God's presence; he had heard the still, small voice in his depths. He had witnessed miracles and watched as an invisible force answered prayers in an eerily supernatural manner. A manner that made him fall to his knees in humble fear of the great Creator and lift his hands in silenced thankfulness. There were moments George had sat in silence and known beyond a shadow of a doubt that God was sitting with him. Now, as he stared into the fiery furnace of hell that awaited him, watching his ill and weakened loved ones having their home—a poor excuse for a home but home nonetheless—ripped out from under them, all the previous miracles seemed to drain from his remembrance. Humans are dangerously capable of validating their emotions; if one is unable to do so himself, he simply seeks the validation of others until it is received. How often had he mistaken his fleshly validation for "the peace of God"?

He had once spoken with a man for hours who passionately believed that God was the manifestation of all the concepts we as humans needed and wanted within our lifetime. Each time prayers were answered, it was either simply what we wanted if we wanted it badly enough, or it was what we truly needed at that time. Either way, it was simply us answering our own pleas. He had explained away every topic of the kingdom of God that George had proposed to him, seamlessly, as if he had placed all his effort in life in the basket of proving God did not exist. He stated that believers were *simply in a state of unawareness mixed with a hunger for purpose, acceptance, and peace.* This state caused them to create a "genie" who gave them a false version of all three: *they were blind mice marching in unison toward the light that just so happened to be a cliff of disappointment they would inevitably tumble off.* He had spoken with pure disdain for those in that category.

George had posed one final thought to him: "Have you ever read Genesis, sir? I assume with your vast understanding of what

Christians believe, you have at least taken a gander at the Good Book?"

The man nodded. "I have read the Bible front to back, back to front, George, many times."

"I suspected as much. And each time you read over the words speaking of how God commanded all of creation into existence—or even the many stories of God demanding nature respond to Him, splitting the sea, sending the flood, the list goes on—did you ever pair any of it with Romans 1:20?"

The man lifted an eyebrow somewhat inquisitively, mixed with a "try me" expression, as if entertained by George's attempt while at the same time bored with the conversation, as no one had been able to budge his opinion since he was old enough to form one of his own. He had assumed it was something he could argue or explain away in an instant; he had no fear of being struck with a challenge that he could not immediately dismiss.

"Romans 1:20: 'For since the creation of the world God's invisible qualities—His eternal power and divine nature—have been perceived, being understood from what has been made so that men are without excuse.'" George paused for a moment, scanning the area around them, taking in the small trees the city had planted, the cracks in the sidewalks, the vital structures that stood within the distance, and the vast sky above them, exhaling as if releasing all cares, his shoulders relaxed, a smile pulled across his face.

He continued, "From structures designed by man, whether they be the large fortresses built in biblical times or the skyscrapers we admire now, to all the trees of the earth, large or small, they all reflect God's nature in such a way that man is quite literally without excuse in the matter of belief in God's existence.

"We look at that scripture and assume it is speaking only of the beauty and splendor of nature, and while that is a portion of what it is referring to, there is much more. It speaks of the demand of God to His creation, it speaks of His care for every fiber of His creation, it speaks of the creativity that flows through the hand of God and into His children, and it speaks of His power, His glory, and His strength. I challenge you, sir, as a stranger whom I met in a park for *no particular reason*, to sit alone and evaluate the world around you. While you do, I dare you to forget your studies. I dare you to forget the reading you have done. Sit with yourself, your true self. Be honest, be fair, be raw as a man, as a human, and sit and watch the world move around you. Let God's power command itself, and even allow the work of Satan on this earth to be revealed to you, and tell me that you do not run out of excuses."

George stood to his feet and with a simple nod made his departure. Standing atop this roof now, George wondered where that man was and if he had ever come to know the Lord; reminiscing on the conversation, he took his own advice. He sat and let his feet dangle. Looking out over all the buildings, cars, trees, and the few people he could make out in the distance, he began to breathe with intention. Each breath relaxed him further. He thought about his life, all the turmoil, all the joy, the people he knew, the experiences he had lived. He turned his focus to where he was right at that moment, feet hanging over the edge of an abandoned apartment complex, the world bustling around him.

Leaves were shifting in the breeze, the trunk of a tree simply just standing, existing. People of all ages roaming the planet. People completely sucked into their plans for the day, hurriedly moving through their tasks. People making big decisions, and others having conversations, laughing, crying, and thinking, just the same as he was. George began to look beyond the surface level of all that lay before him, and soon he wished to be rid of it all.

The mess, the chaos, and the details humans cared so much about that did not seem to make any difference. He felt that if the customs lived out by humans had been removed, they would be far freer to see the existence of God close-up, twenty-four-seven.

Satan has studied humanity from the moment it was created. It is all he seeks to learn about, as it is his main purpose and goal to destroy God's creation. He is out for our heads. He has studied our ways, which truly have not changed since the beginning of time. We feel as though we are innovative and world changers, yet nothing is utterly new on the face of the earth. We can change the world for his kingdom, but there is nothing we do now that has not been done before. With Satan knowing us so well, he executed the placing of a veil over our eyes, removing God from our sight with ease. However, all one need do is seek and they shall find. Simply sit and allow your heart to be open to the possibility of His existence, and He will respond. Any time George faced doubts, he would simply close his eyes and whisper the name of Jesus.

As life goes on and faith grows, the trials tend to hit harder, the enemy seems to bite deeper. This attack was deep enough to cause George to attempt an entirely new way of seeking the

Lord, one he had preached about but never felt the need to utilize. Even when he lost Joash, all he needed to do was simply speak the name of Jesus over the pain, and peace would flow. Not this time—this time he needed to listen to God, watch for Him, to see the evidence of God's heart for His children. This time, George wanted to meet God face-to-face because this time, he was angry. He knew beyond questioning that anger toward God was never valid, as God was right in all His ways, though George, as a man, did not always understand that. Regardless, George felt the need to wrestle it out with God, to manage this turmoil one-on-one with His Creator. With his extremely worn Bible and a trembling hand, he turned to Lamentations.

"'How deserted lies the city! How like a widow is she, who once was great among the nations! She who was queen among the provinces has now become a slave!'" George read aloud with growing frustration, turning his thoughts to the homeless community that he was a part of as well as to all others that flooded the streets of New York, let alone the world. People like him who had once known a blessed life, who had had their opportunities stripped from them, the people who were born into life on the streets. George had been taught growing up that he needed to be thankful for all he had yet have a heart willing to give it all up for the glory of the Lord, remaining in a headspace that God was truly enough, more than enough. Yet now that he was here, living as the "waste" of New York City and about to have even more ripped away from him and his family, doubt began to reason its way to lead his outlook.

He knew that there were at least five who were already sick and would most likely be put to death if they had to travel far enough away from their current space to appease the monsters coming to intrude. Amid his investigation to learn what exactly the Lars were attempting, he had dug up the acreage they planned to redevelop. Two hundred acres, meaning he and his companions would have to travel roughly twenty miles from their location now to be far enough away that those in charge of this movement would not come in response to the scum remaining too close to their new beloved renovations. The chase would be more an extermination: George did not doubt for a moment that the Lars would annihilate his community rather than move them farther away. They were just bugs to those in such a position of power in the city. Better to spray them dead than shoo them away. Marie Lar had chased George out of the building directly following his departure and made it clear that she would not tolerate him or *any of his group of heathens* being within five miles of any entrance to the new city blocks, nor around any other area they had their name on. Meaning it would be a much longer journey than just a couple blocks.

Meaning more risk, being such a large group of *undesirables* as much of the world labeled them, painted a target on their backs the more area they covered. They would have a much better chance if they simply honored that request and made the move rather than standing up against the Lars or any of their minions. They needed to truly be away from New York City entirely. They needed to find a place far more gentle. Safe. George continued to read as these thoughts and realizations of the likeness to his current situation squeezed the life out of his heart: "'Bitterly she weeps at night, tears are on her cheeks. Among all her lovers there is no one to comfort her; all her friends have betrayed her; they have become her enemies. After affliction and harsh labor, Judah went into exile. She dwells among the nations, and she finds no resting place. All who pursue her have overtaken her amid her distress.'"

Tears poured over George's cheeks as he spoke these words aloud, pleading with the Lord in his heart, for what he had not a clue. He felt his gut wrench and desperation flood his insides, but for what? What was he asking of his God? For what was he pleading? For God to stop this transition so his people did not have to leave, for God to carry them as they did leave and to keep them safe on their journey, to simply end their poverty and send someone in to save them?

"Lord, your word was recorded for immeasurable reasons. I cry out as Jeremiah cried out, and I know you will answer with your will for my life, for our life. I hurt, I am angry, and your children are hurting and sick. I know I need nothing but you, but it seems as though you are not sustaining us! Why have you forsaken your people?"

Feeling more rage begin to flourish, George continued to read on, knowing if he changed to his own words for too long, he would simply grow in anger toward God, giving room for Satan to speak his confusion and delusions into the situation. "'The roads to Zion mourn, for no one comes to her appointed festivals.'" Near screaming, George let out his cry. "God, my son would not come to my aid! No one is coming to our rescue, including you! Where is your hand of justice and protection for your children?!" He read on as his sobbing intensified. "'All her gateways are desolate, her priests groan, her young women grieve.'"

A flash of Emilee's face came into view. Her bright smile and contagious laugh brought light and life to the entire community. He heard her cries in prayer almost nightly, her soft sobs filled with gut-wrenching sorrow. Even so, she would end every prayer with thankfulness for her life that day. Unwavering faith filled that young woman to the brim and poured over exceedingly. "'Her foes have become her masters; her enemies are at ease.'" George squirmed at the thought of the vile family sitting comfortably in their castle of a home, sitting on their throne, attempting to rule and ruin this colony.

"'The Lord has brought her grief because of her many sins. Her children have gone into exile, captive before the foe.'" George stopped and closed his Bible. "Yet we have been cast out due to another's sins. We are being punished, it seems, for someone else's crime." His thoughts drifted to Paul's teachings in 1 Corinthians 4:8–10. "'You think you already have everything you need. You think you are already rich. You have begun to reign in God's kingdom without us! I wish you were reigning already, for then we would be reigning with you. Instead, I sometimes think God has put us apostles on display, like prisoners of war at the end of a victor's parade, condemned to die. We have become a spectacle to the entire world—to the people and angels alike. Our dedication to Christ makes us look like fools, but you claim to be so wise in Christ! We are weak, but you are so powerful! You are honored, but we are ridiculed.'"

Though the Lars and all those who collaborated with them to run this city from a place of pure deceit were not wise in anything involving the kingdom of Heaven, the point still stood. They were worshipped in the city's eyes, while George and his companions were spit on only when they dared enter a far more public territory, lest they simply be forgotten. Being forgotten sometimes tasted worse than hatred. If there was a call on their life and a reason for their suffering, George could not see it, nor could others in their group. They all kept faith in the Lord, but none had received a response when praying for the reason God had for allowing their lives to end up in the streets, wasting away, or if they had, they had not shared with the class what the answer was.

Still, this crew of rejected folks knew the Lord Jesus well. In the eyes of their Heavenly Father, they were far richer in their "foolishness for Christ," seeking the power of God to be at work in their lives, than all the world's rich-by-human-standards population combined. Thankfulness for that and not yearning for freedom from the unfruitful roads they roamed was diminishing within George's heart.

He knew he would not be able to redirect the course of his hope by his own strength, his own attempt. He needed to ask God for help to hope. Hope to hope—annoyingly redundant, he thought. It made sense: had humans been capable of gaining unwavering faith and undeniable hope, we would be missing more than half of the Bible. The Lord was the only one who could give him the desires of his heart (Psalm 37:4).

All the psalms were the answer to the cycle of questioning hope and faith. "I have no hope." Ask God for it. "How can I hope in Him giving me hope?" Ask Him for it. The answer was simple: ask and ye shall receive. Seek the kingdom of God, and all else will be added to you. Not a matter of *if*, just of *when*. God's timing was a mystery. Despite the feelings that traveled through his innards, George had to simply pray according to God's word and step back to watch Him release Heaven in response. Standing atop the roof, George permitted himself one final look to sweep over the smog-covered area just beyond their dwelling place, glancing at the towering city in the distance and finally landing on the streets directly below him, the streets his people dwelled among.

"I cannot go back to them alone today, God. I need you to walk with me and bring peace, faith, and strength with You for all of us." George let the plea fall off his lips in a whisper before heading back to his group. Thirty days—*it was a generous offer of allotted travel time.* Thirty days and George had to have all these people moved miles and miles away or else face their extinction. George had no idea how to address this with the large family that sat before him.

Once he returned from his rooftop groanings, he sent the youth to gather everyone for a discussion. The words began to flow from George's lips; he explained the story from the day he had met Mary Ann, as a few of the folks before him did not know the full history, to the most recent moments of repudiation as his son's response to his pleading, as well as the stipulations given by the Lar family as to time allowed and travel distance required. As he spoke, he watched the already sullen expressions grow into an amassed lament from those who had sick family members to care for, along with the removal of any hope remaining in the sick themselves. His heart ruptured at that moment, and for the first time, he broke in front of them all. Tears drenched his cheeks; he became incapable of speaking, and it seemed all the air was sucked from his lungs.

A ringing entered his ears, causing the cries and comforting words surrounding him to fall silent. He finally fell to his knees and just sat as his wife held him, brushing his coarse gray hair, allowing his tears to stain her blouse. The noiseless chaos was finally interrupted, causing the hairs on George's skin to stand straight. A voice of pure exhaustion rumbled through the small crowd.

Amazing grace, how sweet the sound
That saved a wretch like me.
I once was lost, but now I am found
Was blind, but now I see.

'Twas grace that taught my heart to fear
and grace my fears relieved;
How precious did that grace appear
the hour I first believed!

Through many dangers, toils, and snares
I have already come

To this grace that brought me safe thus far
And grace will lead me home.

Nancy, the woman who allowed her worn voice to travel simply yet powerfully through those standing before her, hid in the back, her gaze straight forward at George. She was a wise woman, quaint but strong. If anyone had seen turmoil in their life, it was this woman, who just sent the strongest message these people had heard in quite a long time. She stood crooked from the wear and tear the world had rained down on her walk through it. Slowly she strode to the front, where George remained kneeling. "Young man...do you know the Lord your God?"

Taken aback, as they had all worshipped, prayed, and studied together, George strained a response. "Yes, ma'am. I was just talking with Him this morning. I've been in His presence with you many times. Why would you feel the need to ask me if I know Him?"

The woman grabbed George by the bottom of his chin; though it was lightly, he knew it was with strength, and he dared not move. "My boy, if you know the God that parted the Red Sea, the God that rose Jesus from the grave, the God that can do all we ask think or imagine but does not need to give us anything on this earth but Himself, then why do you appear as though you have been defeated by the one He has already cast out of the kingdom that is your true home?" She paused, removing her hand from his chin and laying it gracefully over her other hand, atop her cane. "I assume you are sorrowful due to it being your son who is causing us to need to travel this distance and leave this scrap of a home. I also assume you are afraid that there are folks in this lot, including myself, that will not make the trek and that our lives are on your shoulders. Does that sum up this slumped despair you are in now?"

George gritted his teeth, shook his head, and grumbled, "My parents brought me out here to escape the poison that is the Peleskes, yet once I knew they were watching me and my family, I should have done more to protect us all. Now my one and only son and the families that set out to destroy me and mine are the force driving half of us to extinction; I failed all of you."

Nancy slammed her cane on the ground, widening George's eyes and stiffening his shoulders in response. "Garbage! Pure garbage! Are you God, George? Absolutely not—you have no capability of saving a single soul if God says it is time for them to come home. The ability you are called to do anything with, by the power of the Holy Spirit, is given solely by God. It is something you receive, not something you own or must bring into existence. You have been faithful to Him, walking in His will, pursuing the kingdom of Heaven from the moment you wake to the moment you sleep. If you are honoring Him, and so are all of us here, and He is allowing this change to happen in our lives, do you not see that it is His will for us? And you being angry about it is you being in direct opposition to the will of God?"

Nancy bent down as best she could to catch George's gaze directly. "Even if He says it is time for any of us to come home, we will make this trek, we will praise Him and glorify Him the entire way, and if any of us leave the earth during that time, it is

His business, not yours. I will not have self-pity get in the way of my God bringing me home if it is my time. You got that?

"As for you stopping the evil that other people choose to conduct via direction from our enemy, did God call you away from us to change those people and stop that evil, or did He call you to remain with us to be a light in this community? Clearly the latter, considering you are still here. The one thing He called you to do involving that family was to seek out your son and request his grace in this matter; you obeyed, and now you let God carry it out. Was it your idea or God's will for you that conducted the outcome of Joash's response? If so, why are you limiting God? He could have a million varied reasons; you just obey and patiently wait for Him to reveal it. Now, I suggest you continue to grieve for a moment, allow yourself to process the pain you are feeling, then pick yourself up and let us start preparing for our walk through the industrial wilderness."

George stood, grabbing his wife's hand with his and placing the other atop Nancy's shoulder. "Ms. Nancy, you are a wise, godly woman. You are the epitome of strength and encouragement. I owe you for the many a time your obedience brought recovery from defeat. Thank you for your obedience to your walk with the Lord and your dedication to these people. You are a mother of mothers. I know that I must take a stand for us all and walk alongside with strength and courage, but I will be honest, I will be real, and I will let you all know this will not be a light or easy move. Let's pack up whatever we can carry in baskets and on the backs of those who can manage it. Any medical supplies you can gather, food, water—you know the drill. Leave as much as you can behind. We will need to head out within the next five days if we are going to make it on time without too much strain placed on our friends who have a hard time traveling. Thank you all for your support. We know the Lord is with us. Keep trusting in Him, and I will work on the same."

Three days coursed by swiftly. On the fourth day, George and Donna awoke facing one another. Clasping his hand in hers and pressing her lips firmly against his knuckle, she looked up at him, attempting to provide a sense of hopeful encouragement; still, he could make out a glimmer of doubt and fear skim across her eyes briefly. "My love, we trust in His will, correct? But do not worry, I am afraid too, so we will just ask Him to calm our fears, and we'll brave this together. Do not allow the enemy to keep you from leading these people to our new home. You were born to lead, you were called to be a light to these—He will strengthen you for that calling. Peace flow over you, my love. Let's get ready to head out."

Her smile still sent shocks of joy through his entire body; the love he had for this woman was unexplainable. He knew without a doubt that God had created her for such a time as this. She would be fine. More than fine—she would be victorious. On day one of the migrations, George, Donna, and Emilee walked through to ensure everyone was gathered and ready to depart.

A doorway, worn, wood chips crumbling from its frame, created one continuous beam of light to reveal a lost-in-wonder Ms. Nancy. She stood, head cocked to one side, eyes closed yet seemingly peering out through the back window with her entire soul.

"Ms. Nancy?" Donna broke the silence with a worried yet tender call to her elder. "Ms. Nancy, it is time to gather up and head out for the first day of travel. Are you feeling unwell?"

"Shh, hush your worries, darling." Ms. Nancy almost sang the words in response. Dust particles danced in the beam of light and landed all around the woman so lost in thought. "Every day I stand in this building before this window, rain or shine, happy or sad, I tie my scarf around my chin and I thank God for the times He has saved me by the tiny hairs that exist on the surface of that chin. Every day He answers me with His peace and His presence. I know He is far more than just this building; I know we have an unfathomable number of moments left together, yet I feel as though this is the end of an experience with Him and I must bid this portion of my life goodbye."

The two women stood in silence a moment longer, soaking in the presence of their Father God Almighty, their savior, Jesus Christ, the Holy Spirit; such a heaviness of His peace could never be taken for granted. Eventually, they gradually made their way back through the decaying door and to the rest of the group, who waited patiently.

"Donna, sweetie, is all OK with Ms. Nancy?" George questioned.

Donna smiled with a curiosity and warmth that already answered him but still chose to speak. "Yes, all is more than well, and I just learned what it means to sit in the presence of the Lord at His feet. After all these years, I get it."

With a quick squeeze from her husband and locking of their hands, they made their way to the front of the group and took their first step out of the barren home they had known for so long, pursuing a place that brought no familiarity. Day by day they would seek the Lord to guide them, protect them, bless them, and keep them in their travels and would trust Him regardless of what lay ahead, despite the enemy.

REUNITING THE FAMILY

Joe's head remained locked forward; he was focusing on nothing, keeping his eyes glued in a trance, ignoring the shuddersome vibrations climbing his spine at the thought of even looking toward the house he would shortly be parked in front of. The home that had fueled his arrogant desire for power sat just beyond his vehicle, and he felt as though he could crawl out of his skin being this close to those who had snared him as a child and used him to their benefit, only to run over any living or nonliving thing that stepped in their way. He knew once he pulled up to the Lars' front door, in his search for George, that the only way to know where his father had traveled was to face those enemies head-on.

I forgive them. I forgive them. God, help me to forgive them. Joe let the prayer cycle through his head, the same one he had repeated every second of his ride back from Baker's Peak. The bitterness had lessened though was still firmly existent. Lifting himself out of the vehicle, he took his first glance at the structure that hid all his childhood memories.

Looking into the window that framed Gideon Lar's office, he came eye to eye with the man he had escaped from into the arms of alcohol. There was that look on his face, the stony look Joash had never seen that man without. With a crack of his neck and clench of his jaw, he strode toward the house. Before his foot hit the first step of the entryway, Marie swung the door open and stepped into its frame.

"Well, I assumed this day would come. Tired of slumming it in the bars, Joe? Come to beg for your respect back? No worries, all is forgiven. All blunders can be erased from the public's knowledge."

Not an ounce of remorse resided behind her stern eyes. Instead, Joe witnessed a flash of arrogance swim across her otherwise lifeless expression. Not a single explanation came to mind to describe the darkness that her speech carried as it reached his eardrums. Therefore, not a word escaped his lips as he simply backed away, prying his eyes from her gaze and turning to head back to his car. He did not know how he would find George, but this was the last place he was willing to be within one hundred miles of now. The strength of the Lord had the power to hold him safe within this meeting; his eyes were on his own strength instead, and he had not enough.

His legs were cement. He could not move them fast enough, as though he were moving through sludge, until *his* voice sniped from behind. "Joe! Come back here, now."

He was stopped immediately in his tracks, not out of obedience but rage. How dare this man demand anything from Joe, let alone expect a respectful response? Turning on his heel quickly, fire shading his neck and face, Joe was on the step, nose to nose with Gideon, within seconds. His aggression caused Marie to shrivel back behind her husband, who though he stood still felt an instant fear ooze from his spirit. Joe said nothing for a moment; he simply stared.

Do not let the enemy defeat you or them; contain your anger. Another thought immediately reminding Joe of the voice he had heard on the mountain, the voice that he was investigating, the one that seemed to belong to the God George had spoken of. Pulling himself back a step, Joe let his eyes close and inhaled a deep breath that begged that voice to stay with him. Finally, he spoke. "Mr. Lar, sir, I do not expect remorse from you, nor do I expect you to understand my fury, pain, and confusion over the choices you have made in this life that have affected me and many others in ways almost as painful as death itself."

The words were flying off Joe's tongue faster than he could produce them. These were not his own words. Still, they continued to flow. "I spent three years wallowing in self-pity, feeling as though my entire existence and identity were lies, battling between returning to this house of lies, deceit, and murder yet immense earthly power and seeking out the God that my true father challenged me to find to stand up to you two and your path of destruction." He fell silent for a moment.

"I see you decided to make a wise choice and ignore the foolishness of that Reis scum." The assumption seethed from between Gideon's teeth; though he spoke back, he held a spirit that remained quite timid.

"It would appear so, wouldn't it?" Joe retorted. "Yet that is not the case. Those years were up days ago. The day I met a stranger in a bar who knew me better than I know myself and longed to destroy me. The day I was pried out of my pit of despair to follow the quest laid at my feet by George Reis. Shortly thereafter, I set out on a journey to discover this Creator he spoke of, to discover the Truth, to discover myself, to see if I had any identity left. I left knowing God and knowing there was no need to stand up to either of you. I have no right to seek vengeance. Instead, I was led to seek forgiveness."

The Lars were sent spinning into confusion at what had been bestowed upon them. "I choose to forgive you two," Joash continued. "I do not fully feel as though I forgive you; I still feel hurt, anger, betrayal, and utter disgust when I think of the paths you have laid in this life. But I *choose* forgiveness. Meaning I am willing to let go and leave this behind me and release you two from any negative emotions, thoughts, or actions on my part. I choose this in obedience to God and for His glory. I release whatever I am capable of daily; the rest I ask God to help me with. I still do not understand all of it myself, but I seem to have this understanding that if I continue to seek the things of God, what I lack in comprehension He will reveal to me. So, Mr. and Mrs. Lar, I forgive you, and I will continue to pray for you."

Gideon scoffed at Joe's statement. "Look around at all we have built; does it look as though we will need your approval, your forgiveness, or your *prayers*? If this is your pathetic attempt to bring guilt upon Marie and me, I suggest you drop it." The arrogance steamed off Gideon's flushed cheeks and puffed chest, provoking a chuckle from Joash. "Something funny, boy?" Gideon snapped and shifted to a deeper shade of red yet again.

"No, Gideon, not funny—unfortunate, though. That you walk in an arrogance backed by nothing but cheating, lying, and hiding behind your minions. One of these days, your eyes will be opened to a man who is the Truth, and I pray it is in time to accept Him into your life. I pray it is in time for your soul to not have to live forever without Him. But I can see at this moment you are not ready to receive that, nor am I going to attempt to force you to. I am still in the midst of accepting Him myself.

"I came here for an entirely different reason. Considering you two were so adamant about forcing George and the community he resides with to relocate, I assume you know where they ended up. All I am here for is that information."

Gideon widened his stance, crossing his arms across his chest. "And what makes you think we would honor any request you have? You are lucky if we do not ruin your name for good. It would take hardly any effort on our part to ensure you would be unsafe to show your face in any area of the US, let alone New York. Demanding something from two people who could end you entirely is not incredibly smart for someone who supposedly has *the Almighty wise one* on his side."

Joash did not allow the defeat he felt to reflect in his stare. Remaining silent, with no idea of what to respond with, he prayed silently. *God, if you are able, please help me. Not sure what to ask, but I need to find George, I need to find my dad.* Before Joash was able to verbally protest, Marie's voice arose from behind Gideon.

"Just give him the information, Gid." Both Gideon and Joe were stunned, sending silence in her direction. "I will not have a scene continue to play on my front porch. He wants to seek out that bum, that waste of air, let him. Let him slum it with the homeless for all we care. It will not affect our position in this city, nor will it hurt our feelings. It is his loss, not ours. He will see quickly, and if he comes back after seeing that the life he had with us is better than this God of his and his trash father, we will own him more than we ever have."

Joe had to admit to himself that stung a bit. This coming from the woman who had wanted a son so desperately that she kidnapped a homeless couple's child to raise him as her own. The woman who had been there through every part of his life just continued to rip his heart open. It was plain to see Marie caught the sorrow her words caused; in response she quickly attempted to move toward Joe, seemingly to comfort him. Her trying lasted a mere moment until a stern arm came down in front of her to intercept her sympathy.

"Maywood, New Jersey. You will find them there. Make it quick. I believe they have chosen to remain in travel. Just remember, we already own them; we could own you just as easily. Marie, let's go back inside. Joe, get off our property."

Joe shifted his gaze between the two but remained silent. He had no words of his own, and no speech escaped his lips from the Holy Spirit. Running his hand down his chin, he turned silently and departed from that front step for what he hoped would be the last time. Once in his car, he sped off without hesitation, pulling over and slamming on his brakes only two blocks away.

His sudden stop was met with screaming horns from other vehicles nearby. Cotton plastered Joe's throat. His pulse was furiously pounding as if trying to escape his skin, and his head seemed to have spun off into an alternate dimension. Not a clue he had regarding how to ground himself; he had never faced such a vast array of emotions with such a rapidly climbing intensity.

Thoughts sparked erratically. *What are you doing, leaving a life of comfort and standing against people who could end you? Just end them; they deserve it.* Joe shook his head in disgust. *Where the hell did that come from?* What was wrong with him that he would ever imagine such horrid ideals? *Intrusive thoughts. Panic attack; I am having a panic attack. That is what this feels like? How do I stop this?* The voice inside Joe's head continued to race with questions as sweat dripped down his forehead and his hands wrung the steering wheel so hard it felt as though flesh were ripping.

"Sir, sir, are you OK?" The voice from outside his window made him visibly jump and recoil. "Sorry, I didn't mean to scare you. I watched you from across the street; since you hit your brakes, I thought maybe you were having some sort of heart attack. Do I need to call 911?"

Joe stared blankly at the stranger and eventually came to enough to roll down the window a crack. "Well, ma'am, thank you for checking, but I believe I just had my first-ever *anxiety* attack."

The woman put her hand across her heart, coupled with an empathetic look. "Oh, honey, you do not need to tell me about those—I get them all the time. You sure you are gonna be all right?"

He was not sure. Was this to be his future? He had lost track of the experiences of nausea, fast heartbeat, and worry engulfing him. Was this to be his normal now whenever he came into contact with trials? This woman seemed to understand, causing Joe to question how many he passed on a daily basis who struggled with panic, stomach-curdling, heart-pounding, and insanity-driving panic. Not wanting to tap into that question with a stranger, Joe smiled at the woman to indicate she did not need to stay any longer; in embarrassment, he wanted her to leave. "Yes, ma'am, I am all right. Thank you for your consideration. I must be going now. Have a good day."

Truth be told, he had no idea if he would recover from this; it had certainly felt as though permanent damage had been done. He slowly closed the window as the woman backed away and methodically pulled back out into the street. He would head home, clean up, pack necessities, and head out to New Jersey. Stifling the effects of his panic until he could speak to George.

Returning home to his mouse hole, it felt still. As if the air had been frozen the moment he left for his climb. None of it felt real. Still, a sense of safety was present. As he collapsed on his sofa, a sigh of exhaustion emptied his chest. Sleep arrested him swiftly before he could jump up to keep himself from drifting. His body released all its tension; his breath grew deeper until even the sunlight slipping out from behind a cloud and pouring in directly over his face did not faze him in the slightest. As the minutes rolled by, dreams drifted into focus. A vision of anxious running, a hunt for George, searching, scouring every hidden crevice of the city. Yet nothing beyond complete failure, as though George would never be found, as if he were too late and this man he longed to reconnect with no longer existed. The nightmare faded to George's face laughing hysterically at Joe's attempt to find him, mocking Joe for rejecting him in the first place. The laughing grew louder until it was deafening. Jolting awake and fully drenched in perspiration, Joe steadied his breathing as reality drifted into focus.

As he looked around his apartment, seeing only what his one night-light could reveal, it finally dawned on him that he had fallen out and had remained there far too long. Joe placed one hand atop his thigh and the other on the edge of the couch to pry himself up to a standing position. Too fast. Pins flooded his skin with mild pricks, and colors danced across his vision. Steadying himself on the arm of the sofa, inhaling deeply, he calmed his body. *What time is it?* Dragging his feet, he moseyed over to the microwave clock: 2:56 a.m. *Shower, then back to bed, an actual bed.*

While waiting for the water to warm, Joe stationed himself in front of his computer, typing the name of the city Gideon had given him. "Maywood, New Jersey." He spoke it aloud to confirm his memory, but the silence seemed to thicken whenever he spoke to himself. Loneliness was quite the tragedy; he had never realized how greatly it affected his spirit until now. It was as if a thin piece of fabric laid over his eyes, blinding him to how miserable a soul he had been prior to his recent days, was now being lifted A thick layer of fog chaining him in denial had now been blown away by a sturdy wind, revealing the real damage underneath. Damage only the Great Physician could redeem.

He could go to a church, he could seek out answers in a library, he could scour the internet—no. It was necessary to learn it from George. The proper introduction to Jesus was meant to be led by his earthy father. Interruption of his skimming through photos of the quaint village, along with a glance at the directions, belonged to the steam rolling from the bathroom door within the ray of light shining out into the darkened bedroom. *Shower and sleep.* A lengthy ten minutes elapsed from the moment Joe stepped into the hot water to the moment he was fast asleep yet again, this time in his bed, with an early alarm set to wake him for the continued venture for discovery.

No nightmares this round; the exhaustion was far too heavy to produce any positive visions, let alone any horrid illusions. On any other occasion, the trees oscillating in the sunlight along his closed eyelids as the wind tossed the leaves about would have woken him from his not-so-peaceful slumber, often after what seemed like a matter of five minutes from laying his head atop the pillow. Now, that same shimmering illumination had no power over his body's willingness to remain at rest.

Joe rolled over to turn off his sounding alarm. Lying back, one arm falling behind his head while the other wiped the gunk from the corner of his eyes, he allowed the task of the day to take hold of his thoughts. *I hope it's not too late, George.* As he swung his legs, planting his feet on the floor, the intimidation of the day pressured him to speak his plea. "God, I need You with me today. This is all to find out the truth, all to determine who You are, who George is, who I am…I am most intrigued, to be honest, about who You are. Because if You are who You say you are, all will be fine. But if You are not…You being who you say You are is driving all hope I have right now. I guess I need your help finding You."

Joe felt quite foolish asking such a thing, still hoping that there was someone on the other end receiving his cries for help; it was all he could ask. Real, raw, transparent, he truly meant what he longed for in his heart. *I need Your help finding You. Your existence does not make any sense for someone who has lived their entire life not acknowledging anything beyond the world in front of him.*

Grit scraped at his face, replacing any dirt with a fresh scent of eucalyptus and charcoal. Cool water in arctic droplets gliding down his skin. A solid scrub of his teeth, a quick comb through dark strands of hair. A basic T-shirt, jeans, and his trusty pair of boots were thrown on without any detailed thought. The routine ended with shutting and locking the door behind him. Gravity alone carried him down the stairs as his mind settled into the familiar yet truly disordered *safe zone*, similar to a happy place as it removed attention from any stress or negative realities raising their ugly heads. In its opposition to happiness, it was akin to a blackout. His mind was simply not connected to a single thought, person, place, or thing. Not reality, not any human, not any responsibility, belief, or idea. He was in a coma yet functioning, if you could even call it *function*. He visited this place often. *Coward.* Joash fully meant his name-calling as an insult to himself as he spit it out in his thoughts, the attack quickly waved away by the carefree safe-zone mindset.

Within moments Joe was behind the wheel, turning the engine and reviewing directions. The world began to whip by in his peripheral vision, the road ahead seeming longer than normal. As in a dream when one runs toward a finish line yet the path simply stretches, making the end impossible to reach. As the pot of gold, this seemed a preposterous treasure, finding this man, finding himself, finding God. The youthful excitement controlling his gas pedal foot was far stronger this time than the familiar cynical voice attempting to self-destruct.

Now crossing into New Jersey along Highway 495, the exact moment he hit land on the other side, his heart began to race. Less than a half hour remaining betwixt he and the town where his father now supposedly resided. His dad, his mom, and his sister. Adopted sister, but to him that still meant something. Heaven knew why—he had not been raised in a family-oriented home in any sense of the term. He wondered if this was a part of himself he got from George. The thought brought a crooked half smile. Truth be told, the relief he felt in no longer calling himself a Lar was more freeing than expected.

Maywood Pancake House. He had finally made it, and the sign announcing food was the only thing that truly caught his attention amid his comatose state. The door had a charming bell that rang as he entered.

The waitress motioned for him to sit wherever he liked. "It's a slow morning, sweetie. Take a seat."

Settling into his booth near a window, he watched as the neighborhood conducted its morning routine. Runners and bikers achieving their fitness goals. Cars buzzing, always seemingly late. A couple sipping coffee, strolling down the sidewalk, hand in hand. *Young love...no, only the second date for sure.*

"What can I get for you to drink, sweetie?" The woman beamed as if it were her honest pleasure to serve others. Her joy seemed uncontainable.

"Thank you for your kindness, I sense peace on you and I need that right now; you have a very contagious joy, ma'am. And I will take a black coffee, along with an ice water, if I may."

The woman chuckled, the kind of chuckle that caused her head to fall back and her hand to land on her stomach. "You know, you are the first young man who has ever complimented me on my *less-than-meek* demeanor with such kind sentiments. I really believe you get out of your day what you put into it. If I walk around glum, or even with mediocre happiness, that is what I am inviting into my day and therefore what I will receive. If I spend my days with undeniable joy, thankful to the good Lord for every microscopic thread of His tapestry, then that is what I will be blessed with in return. Yes, sure, negative moments still happen, but I can remain in joy or return to it after a short cry when needed, even amid pain, if I am constantly pursuing this light-filled mindset. Plus it tends to make others smile as well. I will be right back with that coffee and water."

With a quick wink, a smirk, and a pat on Joe's shoulder, she was off to grab his beverages. Two separate strings of the tapestry, conversation intertwining them; joy the needle sewing away as a woman bustled around in lunch rush preparations, as a man devoured the delicacy that was the Maywood house pancake.

After a while Joe was signing his credit card slip, placing a hefty tip of cash on the table with a note: *Never stop spreading your joy, you never know how it may change someone's life. It changed me today. God bless you.* It had changed him. He ate, and they spoke. Now he could not shake the thought of how his cynicism and negativity had laid out a number of the hardships in his life. At one point when she had gone to the kitchen, he whispered under his breath, "God, I think I know what it means now to count it all joy. Help me to do so just like this wonderful woman you have placed in my path."

Back in the car, the door closed, the key turned, and he was off. Thus far, transformation was taking over at light speed. He feared that meant it was all false; it was far too good to be true. The banter between flesh and spirit increased his exhaustion. His first plan was to find the local police department and ask them about any homeless that might have drifted into their town within the past three years.

The large white building was not too difficult to find. Briskly he entered the establishment before he was able to talk himself down. Strolling up to a window where an officer busily worked on the computer screen in front of him, he nervously knocked on the window. The officer opened it quickly and, without prying his eyes away from the screen, requested Joash to state his needs. This officer's voice and body language screamed exhaustion. He must have pulled an all-nighter, Joe thought. He began to regret bothering this poor fellow with what would most likely be perceived as nonsense compared to what he must deal with daily. Hesitation on Joe's part made the officer, Officer Vogel, turn from his screen to look Joe in the eye.

"Sir, can I help you with something?" he asked with a tired exhale.

"I apologize, Officer, for burdening you with such a question, but I was hoping you could tell me if you have noticed a group of travelers entering your city within the past six months."

The officer's expression quickly transformed into one of confusion and inquisition. "*Travelers*, sir?"

Joash was instantaneously aware of the officer's judgment. He must have looked like an insane conspiracy theorist, and the cop was not about to give his babblings a mere second of his attention if Joe did not quickly explain himself. "No, sir, my apologies, I should have used the correct term from the beginning. I know people who were homeless in New York and had to remove themselves from that area, and I was informed I could find them in your town. If that is not correct or if you are unaware, I will quickly leave, no issue."

"Ha! All right, that makes more sense. Yeah, we had a rather large group pass through a while ago. I am honestly not sure where they go at night, but during the day, they typically hang out around the bridge on Prospect. About two minutes from here. Take a right out of here, drive until you hit Maywood Avenue, then hook a left. Follow that to Passaic Avene, another right there, until you get to Poplar, hang another left, and Prospect will be down on your right a short way. Take that until you get to the bridge. Sounds like a bit to follow, but it is not too difficult to find."

Joe extended his hand to the officer in thanks. "I appreciate the help, sir; it truly means the world. I hope you have a blessed day and get to go home soon." Joe almost sang the gratitude as the elation of the knowledge that George was mere minutes away saturated his entire persona.

"Sure, no problem, man. But can I ask why you are looking for these people? I do not want any issues in my town. We want to be a town that helps the homeless, not harms them." Joash chuckled; in retort, the man simply raised an eyebrow, threatening his seriousness.

"No, sir, I am not bringing any trouble, I promise. My parents are two people that make up that community. Long story, but I just found out they were my real parents three years ago and just accepted the truth now. I need to find them." Joe paused, hoping the officer would not pry any further; he did not want to waste time giving his full testimony at this moment. His heart tugging as though from a magnetic force seeking its match, so he was seeking his father.

"Oh, well, in that case, get out of here and go find them. Just be sure to let me know how it goes. Have a good day, son."

With that, he was back in his original position, working away on this computer. Fumbling his keys into the ignition, Joe could not help but laugh. The pure warmth that filled him from toe to head was more than he could contain. He laughed for the first minute on the road until finally his breath ran out.

The bridge was within view. He knew he was speeding, yet not a care in the world caused him to slow until he reached a designated stopping area along the road, allowing him to park and exit his vehicle. Leaping out of his seat, he began sprinting yet again toward the bridge, looking for any sign of a group of people. No one. Not a single human inhabited the area. He stood catching his breath, looking from the water below to the sky above, hanging his head once and for all in defeat. His pulse, inhale, and exhale were the only sounds that seemed to register as they pounded in his ears.

"Joash?" The voice caused the hair on the back of Joe's neck to stand upright at a force that made it feel as though the follicles would be ripped from his flesh. Slowly turning around, his gaze still firmly planted on the ground until he had made it the full 180-degree distance, he lifted his eyes, his heart dropped to the pit of his stomach, and unwillingly tears began to form. The man he had been severely impatient to see again stood before him with that same stern look.

Only this time, there was also a delight that lay behind the firm structure of George's face, one that flashed only when he witnessed the emotion upon his son's. Stepping forward, away from the group he was leading, George approached his son. "Joash, my boy, my son."

With that statement, the men exploded into a long-awaited embrace. Both allowed tears to fall freely as the moment desperately hoped for had arrived. No words were necessary; the understanding was received equally regarding one another's apologies, acceptance, and love, not leaving out their need to continue life as father and son. To never go another day living separate lives so distant from each other. An end to a life of pain, loneliness, and regret. A beginning to peace, adventure, and *home*.

MEETING THE MR. AND MRS.

A broadened Lismore bottom was threatened with decimation as it met an aged cherry oak in an irate blast. Breath steamed from the flared nostrils of an outraged Gideon. "Worm, pitiful little worm. We saved him from a life of poverty; we gave him power, wealth, a strong name. Yet he allows a sorry excuse of a man, one who could not have raised him with a single ounce of dignity, to get him to turn his cheek from all of this, from us. As though us taking him was such a sin. *High and mighty* now are we, Joe."

The words nearly foamed from the corners of his mouth as veins pulsed in his forehead. Marie, still poised, perfectly silent, peered out of the window at the world. Nothing remotely sinking in or being received at all by her vision. She harbored a numbness that allowed no response to arise to her husband's rampage. Given the chance to turn away from a lifelong con, she was once again whisked away in the gusts of pride. Her feet were the feet that stomped upon cities, families, and lives of plenty to rebuild for profit. The pearls lining her collarbone hung loose most days, but not at this moment.

At this moment she sensed all her sins one by one tightening their grip on the jewelry, pulling it taut against the smooth skin lining her throat. The care it took to raise Joe had distracted her for years from the truth of how she had attained a son. Now as her home had nothing left of Joe aside from his rejection, she felt reality ramming the door of her memories, ready to invade her mind. It would not be long now until the door burst open, flooding this seemingly inhumane woman with an emotion she never dared face prior: *guilt*.

As a barren woman, she'd had to go to great lengths to keep her handcrafted porcelain spotless image bared for the world to view. If they saw one crack, one speckle in her wool, she would be slaughtered. She envied the women who could honestly live by the statement that their identity was not defined by perfection as a wife, mother, businesswoman, housekeeper, and whatever other hats the world expected them to wear. What a joke. She knew no form of love outside of having others fear her reign of control. Fear was fueled into the hearts of others when they viewed you as an entity that could not be defeated. A woman filled with power, control, and pure perfection. Immediately intimidation would rise like a flood around the *others*, nearly drowning them, forcing them to subconsciously bow in the perfect one's presence.

This guilt that rested at the base of her innards must never be revealed, she believed. Guilt admits mistakes. Guilt shined a light directly on the cracked porcelain. She needed a vice, one that she could hide from those it needed to be hidden from yet boast about in front of others. She needed an outlet by which she could release her forbidden regret. She turned from the window and strode silently across the floor of her husband's office. Her movement was quiet enough that she could hear his heart beating in anger. Each step was full of motivation to carry herself through their home to her destination as swiftly as a fox. Eventually, she settled on the floor deep in the basement, her eyes mesmerized by the handcrafted wooden box just removed from beneath a floorboard.

Dainty fingers traced the pattern edging the small treasure chest before pausing under the two front corners of the lid. The token creak escaped two aged hinges as Pandora's box opened. Marie's eyes widened with a deep lust as the rows of neatly packed zipped baggies came into view. Her hand reached forward, pausing for a moment and continuing forward to gently scoop up one of her precious pouches. *It has been a while. Sift the contents. Pour them out. Inhale. Hold. Release. Wait. There it is. Power, confidence, complete control. I am power. I am woman. I am ruthless. All is right.* Slow steps of a maid nearing Marie's territory. As she came into view, Marie felt power jolt through her; this was one person who could know her secret yet would never speak a word out of fear, fear of Marie Lar. A smile of satisfaction slid across her face as the timid woman peered in Marie's direction for only a moment before abruptly removing her gaze and scurrying along with a swift "Sorry, Mrs. Lar, excuse me."

Marie's ego burst to life. *I am intimidation.* She tilted her head back, sensual emotions puppeteering her smirk. She sat on the floor in front of her power source; her beauty, strength, and control pushed her to reign above the woman who had dared look in her direction. *Poor dear, must be entirely demeaning for her to witness a woman embracing her position of power while she stumbles around cleaning up after. Must fuel pure jealousy and self-loathing. I would not dream of it.*

Sinister laughs escaped Marie's lips at the thought, echoing through the halls. Tumbling along the walls, vibrations of wretched humor reached both ears of the maid-turned-momentary-muse. As those ears caught the sound, tears dripped from pupils reflecting the true vision of a cleaning lady's boss woman. As she sprawled across a cold basement floor, residue speckled her skin, dissociation illuminating eyes hardly held open. *And she thought she was the one in control, the one to be envied.* With a wipe of the tears, the house cleaner never broke a stride, removing herself from the presence of such a mess.

Longing existed within this melancholy housekeeper's heart to rush back, scoop up the woman clinging to a displaced hope, and heal her every wound. Yet she remained a daughter of God who knew His voice well, not only knowing how to hear it but also how to obey. "You are not her healer, I am; she is in my hands. Trust me. I will simply use you through your prayer, your kindness, and your serving; the rest is mine to execute." Persuading her feet to hurry her body down the hall away from the cocaine-permeated mess piled on the basement floor, she longed to pray for this woman so broken, but her voice seemed stuck in her throat. Instead, she pushed a cry through her soul, silent, strained, powerful. A prayer that had reached her own ears not yet blasted through the firmament of Heaven. Calling on her Creator, her savior, to send His kingdom down in pursuit of Mrs. Lar, to rescue her from her self-dug pit. *You have done it since the dawn of time; you can do it now.* Eventually, her voice found volume.

"You have not given me a spirit of fear but of power and of love and of sound mind. You have promised to never forsake me, nor any other child of yours, including Mrs. Lar. You heard my cry, and you will answer me. I pray that you would circumcise her heart, oh God, and create a new spirit within her. Reveal yourself to her, soften her heart to you, open her eyes to see who you are, to see her need for you. Revive your daughter, Marie, Lord. In Jesus's name, amen!"

Daylight illuminated beige satin sheets, rays rising to fall on the flushed cheeks of one miserable Marie. Her eyes had opened in her mind at least three times by now, never in reality. Pain pulsated through her jaw and forehead, seeming to glue her eyelids, holding sight hostage. Relief from the pain receded only when the contents of her stomach attempted to climb out of their resting place. Back and forth, a tug-of-war. "Drink. Now." Her husband's booming voice shattered her eardrums.

Placing her palm in his strong hand, which she knew without glancing was held out in assistance, she pulled herself up to lean upon her elbows slowly. "Drink. Clean yourself up. Meet me in the south dining room; you will eat and rest for another few hours. Then we must meet the Holts for dinner at seven. I have silenced all your devices. Do not attempt to turn them back on. We both know that you are in a state the public has no business witnessing, physically or electronically."

Dropping her hand, Gideon spun on his heel slowly and began his departure.

"Do you despise me? Are you trapped in this? Are you as trapped as I am? Has our life been an exhausting waste? Is our marriage wasted? Can this change? I think...I think I need this to change." His wife's words chased his steps quickly enough to lasso his ankles, nearly causing a trip. He stood, a silent statue, center room, facing the exit. Stunned, unsure of how to receive the questions presented to him by his bride. Heavy were the inquisitions traced along the structure of each auricle, slipping in to be heard in a slow, painful pressure. The entire dictionary fluttered around in his mind, unable to land on any branch of his brain to form a tangible retort. His gut knotted in fear. Fear of what? *The unknown.*

Confusion. His wife wanted their entire life to *change*? The adamancy with which her questions were voiced revealed perhaps happiness had left her long ago. Was she onto something? And if so, did her probing initiate an unstoppable force of revolution that would roll through their life, forcing them to throw away all they had built? Whether he wanted it or not, he would be different. They would be different. Could he survive *different*?

"*This?*" He managed to choke out the bullet question as he adjusted focus back toward the woman, tears staining her face. Her expression in response to his seemed a mixture of terror and regret, yet all while she stood her ground in confidence. Her body language informed him he needed to speak more preceding her addition. "This what? This life? This situation with Joe? This *us*? What is it that *needs to change*, Marie? And why does whatever it is need to change suddenly?" His emotion was unease; he was certain he would face loss of control, causing his questioning to burst forth from his lips as anger and nothing less than an overabundance of forced control.

He had towered in every prior situation, but this was a threat to the life that allowed him to be seen as ruler, a king, a force to be reckoned with.

"First focus, get rid of the *power moves*. I have been the woman behind the curtain with you for years. I have witnessed your true flaws and weaknesses, your true areas of power and strength. I have witnessed each portion of your personality that has been apparent in our lives as we have risen in power, stepping on everyone it took to climb to our positions in this city, in this world, and in society. I can see directly through your front. My statements and questions terrified you just now. I am glad. I need you afraid. I believe both of us need to know true fear, the fear of dying knowing nothing real, knowing nothing but murder, literal and metaphorical. The fear of the wake of corruption we have left in our paths and the loss of lives physically, mentally, emotionally, socially, and spiritually that stains our hands."

Marie pulled the covers off her legs and slid her feet over the bedside. Wincing as her temples tightened, she clamored with pain noiselessly. The meat that lined her bones had surely been tenderized. Slight shock ran through her mind when she looked at her skin and did not see the bruises her current soreness should have revealed. But it did not. This had been induced not by force but by slow mistreatment of her body, an internal abuse. All for an hour of *pleasure*. Typically, by now she would be up, gulping her secret rehab smoothie, on her way to the home gym for her private yoga class that would ease her body back into a functioning state. She would be planning her next afternoon of being adored. *Adored—more like envied falsely and hated to the point some would surely end me if given the chance.* This morning she had no focus to improve. Her mind remained fixed on memories of George.

And one gnawing thought. *What if we are the ones who have lived a life of death this entire time? What if none of this matters? What if we're sending ourselves straight to hell?*

It seemed a juvenile question for a woman who had conquered far more second-guessing intrusive thoughts than most. Yet it was the way this thought was entering her mind. Different from any hindrance she had wiped away from her thought life prior. This packed power. It moved her. *How* could not be explained. It moved her nonetheless. She gripped the glass and downed the water provided by her husband. In her entire experience of knowing George, with all the hell that man had faced at her hands and the hands of others, he still proclaimed that his life was a gift from God. That he held joy, strength, protection, and the promise of *life*. Life because of one man he never let go of, *Jesus.*

What American had not heard of the Bible, Christianity, and Jesus? Christianity was the most common religion of their culture. More conflict had risen from these beliefs than from any other religion in the United States. More people felt judged, grew hate, did judge, and based their beliefs on (either for or against) this one faith system. And still, most people in this nation claimed Christianity in some form. It was the faith system that brought miracles. She heard the news most days speak of "only what the doctors would call a miracle." "All we know now is that we require a miracle." Anyone listening knew when the word "miracle" was spoken, only one God would be invoked. These thoughts spun through her mind as the room spun along with them, though she landed on only two questions: *What if my life has been completely wasted not living as though God is real? What if I am technically a dead woman walking?*

"Gideon, come help me up. Let us grab a coffee and sit a moment. While I have witnessed all of your personality, every portion of you that makes up the man I know as my husband, you have done the same with me as your wife. Still, I am terrified to share this with you, as I feel you may no longer love me if I do. So please, listen, be gracious, be patient, and do not judge too quickly." Hearing his wife utter that plea—*Do not judge*—reshaped his emotion from a nervousness to a sense of protection of Marie he had not felt recently enough to recall. If she cared enough to request a lack of condemnation, her focus of discussion must have been one far more detrimental to her mind and emotions than any other conversation the two had had in their years together. Immediately he rushed to her side and, without a second thought, scooped her whole body up into a cradle, carrying her to their sitting space. Her face shared a jolt of confusion initially; it had not been long since the last time her husband had touched her, but it had been years since he had touched her like this. With compassion, care, and honor.

As if swooping in to be her hero during destruction. He did well at it. In the moments between a slept-in bed and this serene seating, it felt as if time had paused or simply slowed. As her ear received the pulses of his beating heart, a flushed cheek lay upon an oak chest. *Tranquility.* Bliss remained present as her husband lowered her down into the chair. Keeping her eyes closed, she gave him a soft smile and lay her head against the tall velvet seat back. As he pulled away slowly, allowing her grin to grip his heart, they gave each other's hands an intimate squeeze. *Intimacy like this, I have missed it.* The thought fluttered past the minds of both husband and wife.

She remained in her peaceful state, listening to his shoes travel toward the hallway. He peered down the hall, hoping to catch the maid Lilly, who always brewed a magical cup to their exact liking as if she were the queen of coffee. "Oh, Ms. Lilly!" he called in a yelled whisper. "I am so sorry to bother you amid your break—this may sound silly to you, I suppose, but I believe one of your coffees would significantly impact this conversation between Marie and me. Could I bother you for two cups? I have a deep intuition that this morning may bring heavy conversation. Life-changing conversation."

Ms. Lilly stood staring as a deer in headlights; this man had never been rude to her per se, but this level of compassion was one she had never met from Mr. Lar. "Oh, excuse me, sir, pardon my hesitation, yes, of course, it would be my pleasure. Would you like them in the sitting area?"

Gideon took her hand in his and gave her a look most endearing. "Yes, Ms. Lilly, that would be splendid. Thank you."

Thankful and timid, she removed her hand, turning to click-clack her way to the kitchen. Her heart was confused at her boss's new demeanor, yet she rushed to honor him in such a state in hopes that her respect and swift response would encourage this version of him to return. Gideon strode softly back toward Marie; as he rounded the back of the chair to face her, two emeralds revealed themselves, peering up at him with gratitude and, still, a slight uneasiness, considering the discussion that was about to unfold. Years of secrets, deceit, *pain*. It had taken its toll on both, though they had never broken the outer vase to reveal the decay within until today.

Today brought a glimmer of hope. The knowledge that within the two of them resided even a spark of regret for the catastrophes they had caused, a spark of hope to remove themselves from this life of obscurity. Although even as Gideon now knelt before Marie, seated in Victorian velvet, listening to her breath, to the tick of the clock, rounds of the minute hand, fear still gripped their hearts. At this moment they were husband and wife, strangers, and neither. Only opening the box of dialogue would tell. Schrödinger's couple. Two pairs of desolation-filled pupils having witnessed each other in every light imaginable within their years of being wed, with the exception of a brilliant illumination such as the one that had descended at this moment, now resting among a soundless four walls. The light of admitting the pitiful truth that their success had come with mistakes that had ripped through lives as a natural disaster would tear the earth.

Echoes of Ms. Lilly broke both stares and quiet. The Lars turned their attention to their housekeeper, taking the coffee from her with care. "Thank you, Ms. Lilly. You are free to take the rest of the day. Tell the rest of the staff as well—all can take today to rest, with pay. We appreciate you."

Marie had not one thought before speaking; words simply rolled, a gift that seemed long overdue, held in prior by the demons of domination. Shock lined all three expressions. A response came to Miss Lilly quickly this time, with a slight giggle. "Oh, thank you, Mr. and Mrs. Lar. Thank you. I will tell them."

Before the two could utter a response to her gratitude, Lilly was across the floor and through the exit. Gasps of excitement began to travel their way through the halls as the staff was informed of the morning's gift so graciously bestowed. Marie and Gideon turned their gazes from the hallway toward one another, stunned expressions still lining their faces, finally breaking out in laughter upon their unspoken mutual realization of incredulous amounts of joy over such a menial opportunity to simply *take a break*. "The evidence of our cruelty ripples through so many areas…yet we can still find laughter." Marie's announcement silenced any amusement from the two. "I remember the look on Donna's face. I remember the look on all their faces. I recall the way their bodies looked…I recall turning my sorrow for them into judgment almost instantaneously.

"Their looks of hunger instantly became—*should have been more prepared for our original attack*. If they had been as sly and as powerful as we, they would not have been in this predicament. My thoughts continued like this the entire visit and a long while after. As the years passed, I was able to silence any thoughts of them altogether. Until now. Now all my suppressed demons have clawed their way to the surface."

Gideon stayed silent while transitioning from his position in front of his wife to sitting in the chair beside her, giving him access to eye contact at her level. He stared, wordless, searching for a response; the possible responses seemed to be fluttering through his mind, hummingbirds, impossible to capture. Yet time, focus, and a patient wife granted him the opportunity to finally formulate a reply. "I cannot say I do not feel sick even having this discussion. It is as though you were smacked in the face with a Bible and it left an imprint, but for what, mere seconds of our life? Forgive me, I do genuinely care that you seem pained and burdened."

"All I have in this life I would toss away in one breath if it ever meant you would be taken from me if I failed to do so."

"I am not an unintelligent man; I see my wife sitting in front of me, I can read her face, and though she has not spoken much, I still believe I comprehend where this conversation is leading me. Tell me if I am incorrect—you feel as though we are bad people. We have lied, stolen, murdered, albeit indirectly, and we have hurt people directly by ruining their lives to improve ours by any means necessary. Now you feel guilt and shame for all the *bad* we have done, the crimes we have committed, and what? Did you want to give it all up? *Change our ways?* No lying, stealing, hurting, cheating, et cetera. You want to be *good people* now?

"What if that requires us to lose all we have attained? I understand there are *good people* who live the lifestyle we do, and I assure you that is a miracle for them. I question whether or not we want to risk all that we have for the opportunity for a miracle to fall upon our lives. Miracles require faith, I assume, and 'God.'

"We renounced that a long time ago, and now we are just supposed to become *God people*? Do you even know what that looks like? Are you prepared for the drastic changes in our lives if we suddenly try to become martyrs? I am not attempting to mock you, believe me; I am truthfully expressing to you my concerns."

Looking down at the cup in her hand, she shook her head as her response fluttered out quickly. "Gid, I do not know how to explain this. Ever since I looked into his eyes, George's eyes, and heard his voice, it was as if someone else had entered the conversation. It was a presence that I cannot shake the memory of. Existing amid that presence brought emotions—guilt, regret, fear—of what, I was not sure at first. But more than those, it brought a longing to have the darkness fall off me and to remain in that presence continuously. It was like a hunger to never leave that place but to simply let my stains, which I had not seen before that encounter, be cast out of the space I resided in with who I assume to be God. I have watched movies, and I have heard others talk of things of this nature. I am always shrugging off the topic as babblings by radical *Jesus freaks*.

"Yet now that I have tasted it, I know in my core there is no other explanation. So, to answer your question, yes, I want *out of the bad and into the good.* That sounds laughable and like a *silly* cliché, but I do not know how else to word it. I can see now that we have been walking hand in hand with the devil himself and that has me shaken to my core in terror. How we walk this out I have not a clue. We cannot undo the bloodshed that lines our palms. We cannot take anything back that has been done. Yet I want out of this coat of shame, and the only way out, it seems, is God…I only know He exists because I have walked so close with Satan that there is no doubt of His existence.

"So where do we start? I think we need to find a pastor. There is a church I've heard of that is starting to grow significantly. I want to go there."

Marie moved to kneel in front of her husband, taking his face, still strong and sturdy, into her delicate fingers, running her thumb across his cheek as she shifted her gaze, tracing his expression.

"Listen, Gideon, all I ask of you is to stand by me. I do not ask you to understand or to comprehend the presence I speak of. I had no understanding until I felt it myself, and I still have so many questions. I am not asking you to miraculously realize that you require change or to cover yourself in shame. I am simply asking you to walk alongside me as I seek this out. Come with me to talk to the pastor. That is the only task on my heart at this time, so that is where we will start. If you are willing to stand by me."

Gideon reached down and scooped his wife up into his lap. His fingertips shifted a loose strand of hair from her face, tucking it behind her ear. "I will stand beside you amid fire or rain, joy and pain. I will rise and fall holding your hand. I will walk, I will run, I will crawl as long as I get to stand beside *you*." He paused, placing a long kiss atop her tear-stained lips. "Out of all the horrid lies that have left my mouth, Marie, that is one truth I have stood by since I spoke it to you on the altar. When do we leave, my dear?"

INVITING THE LORD

Joash freed his father from his grasp, but not before the embrace bonded two strangers into family. Son met father's stare as he backed away, witnessing the joy flowing alongside and undertone of curiosity. Joash patted the questioning shoulder and spoke before *What are you doing here?* could be uttered. "I came to find you...I have questions; I think maybe God led me to seek you out. I know I could have gone to a pastor or any other random Christian, yet I believe I needed this to be between you and me. That is, if you are willing and have the time."

Investigation left George's thoughts instantly. Mild shock replaced half of the removed emotion; the other, sheer gladness. "Joash, I have spent years reminiscing about memories I never made. Playing catch, reading the newspaper together before work and school, teaching you how to make the world's messiest sandwich, driving, shaving, your first heartbreak. All of which I work to not live to regret, as regret would mean that I have a lack of trust in the plans our God is going to execute through this very unusual life we both have experienced. Yet I still revisit these pretend memories from time to time to feel connected to you, my son. Do you want to know what I play through my head the most?

"Teaching you about your Heavenly Father, Yahweh. Introducing you to your Lord Christ Jesus and instructing you on how to remain in the Holy Spirit that lives within you. This is my purpose in your life, son, to disciple you. It is my honor."

Donna's voice broke through their conversation. "Well, boys, from the sound of it, you two need time to sit and begin a hefty discussion. I see a park bench just over there that would be perfect. In the meantime, the group and I are going to determine our next meal. If you need us, we will be headed a couple of blocks over to talk with the restaurant owners." Donna paused, meeting her son's gaze, the eyes that had once looked to her for life so briefly now still saying, "Mom, I need you." She held back no longer and threw her arms around her boy in a long-awaited momma's hug, bringing both to tears. "OK, enough of that— you two have much to talk about," she said, releasing her son, wiping drops from under her glossy eyes with the fabric from her shirt.

"I love you, Mom. It is good to be home; you are my home. As unrealistic as it may seem considering our quite irrational and impossible circumstances, your presence is the only place that I have ever felt I could call home. Even having only been in your presence once in my life that I can truly remember. Now, that does not mean I am going to move out of my home to live under a bridge—but that is because I plan to see to it that the rest of you do not remain in a homeless state much longer either. With that said, here is my card; use it to buy the entire group whatever they are hungry for. I have frustrations, doubts, hopes, and questions that need answering, so it may be a while. I will do my best to return him in one mental piece."

Joash gave a slight chuckle at his mother's eyebrow-raised expression of gratitude, shock, and a little worry. Despite the years separated from him, she was still capable of sharing the "mom look" at a moment's notice. They departed from the group, with deep sighs released, the only noise amid held tongues. Their voices caught in their throats, unsure of how to begin, one anticipating excitement to teach, one attempting to discern the multitude of thoughts arguing *the point of this all* within himself. George knew he could not be the one to begin the conversation.

They would sit in the quiet as long as Joash needed to begin his inquiry. Joash wanted to be rescued, but he first needed to gain enough humility to admit the truth aloud. *I could simply go back; I could simply ignore the voice and presence experienced on Mount Baker. I could easily explain such a phenomenon as one's mind becoming a god in a time of severe need of a savior.*

Despite teeter-tottering, he said, "Listen…I have no clue how to begin. As a man who has denied the existence of God and refused to lend an ear to anyone claiming *Jesus is Lord* for his entire walk of life, now suddenly having experienced an encounter that seems to be explained only as the one I've rejected speaking directly to me—how to even look toward God after these years? How to completely drop the beliefs I have had since birth? It is all rather strange. It would be much easier to return to normal. Simpler. Much simpler." Joash spoke with speed and force as if it took all the effort he could muster.

"Simple. Yes, Joash, simple it would be. So why don't you?" George prompted lightly, sternly, and with sincerity. Joash turned his face ninety degrees toward his father, raising a challenging brow. "Do not take offense—it is merely a question, one to which you will most likely find answers. Going back is simple, you say, so why don't you? Just think about how you would reply to that for a moment, Joe."

Joash retracted his pressing posture, squaring his shoulders forward, sinking into defeat. Clenched jaw lifting toward the heavens. Lids squeezed tight, forcing pupils to remain untouchable by light. One large gulp failed to swallow the pain crawling up a dry throat. "Because once you encounter Him, you cannot unencounter Him. Listen, I have faced pain within the last few years that I never expected. I would face in my lifetime. It began with an attempt to ignore that I did not belong to Gideon and Marie and had other parents out there. I had myself convinced, to be honest. That the money, the power, and the worry-free lifestyle were all worth the choice to sweep under the rug any thought of you or anyone else that could not benefit my *reign*, if you will. Yet there remained a gnawing at the back of my head. At first just a tiny poke, like the nudge of a mouse tapping. But it grew into a rat trying to pry its way through the bone of my skull. *You cannot ignore this. Your life has been a lie. You might as well not exist. Nothing you have can save you from being a pawn in the game of the Lar family. Look at all the destruction that was visited upon the lives of others, all for two humans who used your existence to manipulate the world to bow down to them."*

Joash paused in an attempt to hold back tears that were begging to pour from reddened ducts.

"Let it go." The words came in a whisper from beside him, and he listened. Joash began to weep and shake, releasing liquid sorrow in amounts far surpassing those that he believed existed within his torn soul. His mind was a whirling twister of emotions; he could not control the collapse into his father's lap. A grown man, lying sideways on a park bench, sobbing in the arms of his dad. Not one care swept over Joash as he bared his hurting spirit to the entire park surrounding him.

"Why is letting go an act that brings such agony?" Joe demanded.

George carefully assisted Joe to a seated upright position; Joe's elbows rested upon his knees, and his head found comfort face down in his hands. "Joash, there are two answers to that question that come to mind. One, there has been pain and suffering brought into our world through sin and Satan, yet we were made for eternity in a kingdom that rejects all sin and the devil himself. Naturally, anything that opposes our divine purpose is going to be painful. We were created with the spirit that refuses darkness, yet we have a flesh that at times invites it. Two, we have a powerful enemy that is quite literally hell-bent on destroying us.

"He has tools—shame, fear, deceit, pride, lust, hurt, offense, control, manipulation—all of which make us long to keep our darkness hidden. They tell us the lie that if we allow ourselves to be vulnerable and honest, we will die. It may sound drastic, but at times the truth is just that. Drastic."

"I need to move; I cannot stay stagnant in a discussion like this. Honestly, I am certain it is because I have not had a drink in long enough that now withdrawal is beginning to anger my body. I still face this from time to time. Can we walk?" George stood to his feet and nodded forward in response to Joe's agitated request. "Thank you. At times, to complete a thought, I need to move. I have been that way since my teenage years, though it did worsen with my alcoholism. I am not entirely sure how to continue the conversation after such a humbling break. Walking will help."

Joash had never before been able to put his state of discomfort into an explanation, much less share his heart out loud. The two strode side by side silently for close to twenty minutes before Joash was able to speak. "There is a war I am facing. And it seems as though it should be an easy enough war to win. I thought I had won it prior, anytime faith in a *higher power* or questioning my morals came into play. Yet this round is unfamiliar.

"Nowhere in my mind feels safe anymore. I continue hoping that any moment now, all that has played out since the day you walked through the door will be taken back as if it were a movie and now, having seen an intrusive thought play out, I could hit rewind, confirming those events did not truly take place. Although then what would I be? A grown man high on power, staking his claim over all he hungered to seize, carrying the name of his true enemies hidden as his closest relationships?

Being fooled by snakes in his own house? Fool. That is what I would be if I wished to remain in the dark. I must be a fool."

George paused his steps, inhaling deeply, releasing his prayer through the air, a test before speaking aloud, carefully, and thoroughly seeking God's confirmation that his discernment was indeed correct.

"I do not want to speak out of turn, and I do not believe I am; feel free to challenge that if you must, but I have an inkling that while you do not feel safe in your mind, nor at home with the Lars, there is one place in this large world you do feel a sense of safety. However, reaching out for that specific buoy means a leap of faith that would cause you to release nearly every other idea that has made up who you are. Grabbing that hope, that hand, means leaping from the only pedestal you have ever been grounded on in your entire walk through life." George's words fell over the ears of his son, who held still as carved clay for fear he might miss one of those precious words. "There is a deafening fear when you gaze around at the world you once knew," George continued. "You feel as though the *truth* you once knew and lived is now backing you off a plank into raging seas. Yet there is another path creating a bridge for you. Half of you longs to step onto that bridge and be connected to the architect. Half of you has an unease regarding that bridge leading to a life you do not fully understand. A life you know nothing about. A life you have abruptly rejected until now. Does this sound correct?"

George stood, still at a slight distance from his son, patiently waiting for Joash to receive what had just been spoken.

"What if the voice I heard, the elation I felt on the side of that mountain, was simply human? What if I was so broken and struck with withdrawal that I was giving myself responses that I longed to hear deep inside? What if I was subconsciously spiking my serotonin to levels I had not previously released and that was the *presence* I felt? I could take a step onto this bridge, as you say, and reach toward its builder and be reaching for a false ideology that all along was a power coming from within my soul. I could reach and find there is no one to catch me; I could fall into the crashing waves and drown. Or I could reach, and a hand could be waiting for me to guide me through, and I could accept that there is in fact a Creator to lead me in my true identity from here on out. Two drastically different outcomes. No definitive proof for either. So which path to choose? That is the war."

"Two challenges to that, Joash. One, Jesus is a person. You know that now because you called on Him in spirit and in truth on the side of that mountain. Can you honestly pause and say at this moment in time you do not know that Jesus is a person? If so, you're arguing with history. So we know Jesus is a real person. Can you also ignore that you can say from experience He is alive and well?

"Two, on the mountain you were desperate, searching for answers, so of course you could chalk that up to it just being a response to your sheer hunger for peace. Yet at this moment, you are seeking ways to deny God's existence because it is frightening to step out on a ledge of believing without physically seeing. But you can sense Him still. Can't you? You can no longer remove or deny the acknowledgment that He exists, can you?"

Joash let out a flustered chuckle, jerking his head back and pressing his hands to his face, finally dropping them to rest on his hips. "No. No, I cannot. It is as though I am now permanently aware of Him. As if He is consistently speaking to me, even without words. And I want to know more. More of Him, more about what He has to say to me. More about what life with Him is like. Yet I feel angry at Him, honestly. Why did He not reveal Himself to me sooner? Why did He allow me to be taken? I may not truthfully be questioning His existence anymore, but I sure have questions about His tactics in my life. Christians say that He is good. In my core, I sense that to be true, but with my eyes, I've witnessed things that cause challenge to arise on the topic of goodness."

"My boy, already you have a good quantity of deep-ended questions; I assure you that is just the beginning of your interrogation of Heaven. You know, though, you do. You know the answers to each. They are hidden within your core, within the wisdom God has begun to bestow upon you and will continue to grant you in response to your seeking Him. You get to choose each answer you receive, however. Will you allow anger, opinion, self-righteousness, and more to silence the voice of the Holy Spirit you have now awakened to? Or will you push past the self-taught knowledge and doctrine to dive further into *the* Truth above *your truth*? Choices, my son. Our days are made up of a million microscopic choices. Take them one at a time."

George's God-given wisdom poured out over Joash's heart as precious honey. Joash straightened up to face the challenge. "First question, the same question I have heard many folks ask and answer throughout my years observing the world. If God is so good, why all the bad? Why allow my parents to be driven out by evil? Why allow me and the Lar family to sow all the dark power over this nation? Why allow me to drift into alcoholism, despair, and suicide attempts? Let us not mention the countless stories in the Bible that tend to paint Him as a God who breathes fire over His own creation for not being perfect. How is He good when all of this exists?"

Joe's questions had arisen calmly at first yet ended in gritted teeth and a heightened volume. Still, his father chose a gracious response. "We reap what we sow. I know that is a very cliché response. However, it is packed with more Truth inside it than what meets the eye. Just as a seed is packed with more power than we are typically capable of understanding. Do me a favor. Sit and close your eyes." George made his way to the ground, lay back on the grass, and patted the spot next to him, inviting his son to do the same. Joe looked around at those passing by, spending their day outside in the sunlight. A fleeting thought passed through his mind. *This is absurd. What will others think? What if they come over and ridicule us? Is there any real purpose in this anyway?* Once again, he heard the calm voice from his dad: "Let go."

He must have sensed my apprehension. With a shake of his head and a huffed "What do I have to lose?" Joe lay beside his father amid the bright-green blades.

"Thank you for humoring me. Now, picture a large field of flowers as far as the eye can see. As many bright colors as you could possibly envision. Now, picture trees—tall, bright-green leaves and strong trunks. Including animals, roaming. Animals of every kind, even those you would be amazed to see in the wild. Picture a sun so perfectly shining or rain so beautifully flourishing, whichever appears clearer in your mind.

"Imagine peace. Imagine all being well with you and all creation before your eyes. Now, visualize in your spirit that presence that you experienced on the mountainside quite literally being directly next to you in this *Eden*. Your Creator is standing close beside you. Pouring His love into your heart as He walks with you. Are you aware of all of this? Are you in this place, Joe?"

Tears began to slowly form, rolling down Joe's temple. He spoke not a word in response to George's question. Silence was the answer. A talent he was becoming quite familiar with, speaking soundlessly. George's heart leaped with joy that his son was receiving what God was calling him to speak, pushing him to continue. "Good. Now, in this place, are you afraid?" George probed.

"No. Not afraid. I feel as though I am about to have the soundest rest of my days," Joe whispered.

"I am glad. Unfortunately, now we have to take a turn. Picture a temptation. Be it alcohol, lust, etcetera. Picture that urge that draw. Imagine you slip and take a sip. That sip was the one thing your Creator, your Peace Giver, the Lover of Your Soul, instructed you *not* to partake in. The devil has now sown the first seed of betrayal through you, temptation, sin, darkness, chaos, confusion, lies. Your eyes have also opened to how to grow the seed you planted. You knew in the beginning how to water and grow the seeds of the kingdom of Heaven; your Father created you with that wisdom. He hid from you the knowledge of how to fuel your sin. Until you chose sin over Him. Now that

that protection is removed, the choice becomes far more difficult between watering the things of Heaven or hell in your life.

"You are now far more susceptible to feeding the things of Satan that tempt you through lies and deceit as to how beautiful the flower will be in your life. Yet it is a sham. Inside, that flower is rotting from the roots up; you are blinded to its true nature. Regardless of whether you plant and water that seed, it will grow and it will take root in your life. Its disease will spread to other plants in your garden as well as the gardens of others until you decide to pluck all sin out of your life and begin to sow the seed of Truth, the heavenly seed that is the word of God.

"You see, all this evil that you see is simply a by-product of human after human planting, watering, and growing the seeds of hell in this world, blinded by the true nature of what the seed held, deceived that the seed of Heaven was *actually the harmful plant, that that plant will not satisfy you, that plant is controlling, suffocating, contradicting, fake.*

"Could God immediately wipe away all of our want to sin? Could He immediately remove all desire for evil and therefore destroy all the rotten seed that has germinated in our world? Of course. He has the power to do infinitely more than we ask, think, or imagine, and to Him be the Glory for it. Ephesians 3:20–21. Remember that scripture; visit it later.

"However, When Jesus hung on that cross, between the moment of His last breath and His resurrection He legally became the worlds worst sinner in existence simply so He could take sin to the grave and leave it there for good. It is finished. Yes we still have to walk out this life and choose His gift. His blood bought freedom, His redemption, and His saving hand are gifts. Gifts that are held out for all. All have the gift of forgiveness, redemption of soul and surrounding life, abundance, peace, and pure joy. It is extended to the world, excluding no one. The single thing we are required to do is choose to accept. I am certain if you truly look back through your memories, you could pick out moments in your life when God was extending His hand to you and you willfully swatted it away in rejection. Rejection of Him is what led to evil running our world in the first place. I understand that may be hard to admit because we believe we have such little power in our relationship with God. We are just human, right? Wrong. He yields access to the power of the kingdom of Heaven to us daily by offering us the gifts of Heaven and empowering us to choose Him or ourselves. If we choose ourselves or Satan, we do not get the benefits of Heaven. We still have His Love. That is freely given regardless of your choices. Love, Blessings, and Gifts are not one and the same. Love is unconditional; blessings and salvation are not."

With his eyes held closed, Joash momentarily meditated on the journey his dad's words had just brought him through. "I knew there was a reason I specifically had to find you and not simply seek out any preacher or pastor. There was a *calling on my spirit*, I guess, that told me you would be the one to answer my questions in a way that I could truthfully comprehend. That you were the only one to bring new knowledge into my line of sight and help me receive said knowledge and grow it into wisdom. I know this to be true because you are the only man who can provide the dad I have always needed. Making you the only one capable of introducing me to the Heavenly Father."

George grasped his son's shoulder. "Joash, it is an honor I will not take lightly to walk this out with you. You have a fresh understanding of who God is and of the gospel of Jesus Christ now, correct?" George posed the task-required inquisition as his stomach churned with hope for his son's salvation.

"To my utter shock and downright unexpected revelation, I do. I can say truthfully there is not one part of me that could *honestly* deny that God exists, that He gave me life, and that through the death and resurrection of Jesus, I have the opportunity of salvation and life everlasting. I may have no clue what that looks like or what my walk with Him will entail; I just simply cannot deny knowing the Truth of the gospel any longer."

Joash could feel change encircling his body; he could nearly taste a transformation happening within his mind, amid his heart and soul.

"Well, scripture tells us that there is only one way to accept and receive the salvation freely given to us by God through His son. That is, we believe in our hearts and confess with our mouths that Jesus is Lord and repent of our sins. Are you ready to take that step?" George sent the offer with growing anticipation.

"See, the only word in there that has me teetering is the one and only 'repent.' I do not know how to just stop being all the things I am not supposed to be. I am unsure if I can make the promise and stick to it that I will one hundred percent rid myself of sin and fall in line with obedience in every choice, word, action, and thought that has yet to come in my lifetime. That task seems impossible," Joe retorted.

"Well, bud, when you put it like that, yes, that is impossible. You see, you misunderstand the word 'repent.' It is a turning of the heart, a statement: *God, I am choosing to now submit to you as Lord. I long to obey you and am willing to allow you to mold my heart and make me righteous through your guidance, correction, and word.* It is simply a willingness, Joash. A willing choice to acknowledge what is sin, what is righteousness, and to pursue the kingdom of Heaven above all else.

"You will never be completely sin-free; you will fall and falter. A righteous man falls seven times. When you trust in Jesus and choose Him as Lord of your life, you will be picked back up and guided back to the path you chose when you welcomed Him into your heart. He offers salvation to everyone, which means everyone that has ever existed or will ever exist was designed with the ability to, with the help of our Creator, walk the walk of faith. Including you."

George paused and held his breath for his son's response. A sweeping breeze filled the air with scents of blooming life. Seconds ticked by as one man began to let go of fear and choose the narrow path of following a carpenter, a friend, a savior, the one Truth, the one path. "I'm ready."

Both men bowed their heads in a prayer, inviting the lover of their souls into Joe's longing heart, son repeating after dad: "Father in Heaven, thank you for Jesus. Thank you for the salvation I can freely receive through His sacrifice on the cross. Please forgive me for all my transgressions. Please help me to forgive those who have sinned against me, and please help me to forgive myself. I invite you, Jesus, into my heart; I submit to you as Lord of my life. Please come into my heart. My heart and my life now belong to you. King of Kings and Lord of Lords, may I never turn back from knowing you. In Jesus's mighty name, amen."

INITIATING THE
INTENTIONS

The pair had made their way from the park back to the restaurant to join in fellowship with the now full and grateful members of the community. Celebration ensued with another meal well deserved for the group of homeless yet miraculously thankful souls, as well as a celebration of salvation received by a newly proclaimed child of God. Laughter grew and drew the attention of the staff at the restaurant. They became curious, longing to hear the tales of this crew. The questioning, though, would never be spoken. Manners did abound. Instead, they simply listened from afar, scooching in closer to the group carefully so as to not draw attention to their eavesdropping. As Joash, George, and Donna began to reminisce about their testimony, tears arose among the staff as well as others who had entered the premises seeking a tasty treat. More movement and inspiration were received by those who permanently inhabited the quaint yet Holy Spirit–barren town as He moved through the words and stories of these strangers, ringing in their ears with promises of hope.

Nestled in a corner booth, remaining skillfully invisible, one young woman sucked in each word as if starving to hear. Simultaneously recording each delicious decibel in a notepad filled with stories that had each caused her to lengthen her deliberate game of hideaway with her boss. Her boss was playing unknowingly. All he knew was the lines she fed him about a "family emergency" that required her to visit home so she could "handle" it and return "ASAP" with a completed "scrumptious" project "perfectly primed to print." What a line that had been. Home was a frequently mocked idea. Mocked on the surface. Longed for at her core.

She'd woven in and out of houses through a broken system, never once landing in a home. Left at a firehouse, her mother discovered dead, a heroin overdose, only a few mere steps away in the nearest alley. Her father discovered nowhere. She watched others in their neat little bubbles laugh with their loved ones. She watched them be *home*. Sitting in an old tree in Columbus Park, she could see into the lit windows of apartments nearby. Her favorite, a young family, mom, dad, three kids.

They did not have much, though the joy plastered across their faces as Dad chased them down in pursuit of tickling toes before bed made them the richest crew in the city. Often she would close her eyes and be running alongside all of them, snatching her brother and helping Dad to get his feet. Then she would kneel beside them at bedtime and pray to Jesus, "The Lord is my shepherd, I shall not want. He makes me lie down in green pastures." She had no idea what that meant, but she longed for this Jesus to find her, scoop her up, and carry her back to His flock.

It did not take her long in life to realize journalism placed you close to people, close enough that she could continue to pretend she was a part of something. Only you had to last, and to last you must have talent, you must sniff out the juiciest stories before the next team did. She had never won out, aside from mediocre pieces on teen car theft. In New York, that meant she had nothing. Until now. Now she had nearly all the ingredients for the journal entry in a matter of moments by sitting in a diner in an off-the-wall town. *There must be a God.* All she needed now was to piece together minimal underlying details. What was recorded thus far was unquestionably moving. Yet it lacked proof of a scandal.

October 23, 2014. "The Lost Boy: A Hidden Scandal in the Heart of New York."

- Joash, a boy separated from his parents—but how? They haven't shared that detail yet. They've shared so many other portions of the story; why is that held back?
- Donna and George are the real parents of Joash—so who raised him? He's roughly in his thirties, so where has he been his whole life?
- The group, including Donna and George, are homeless, but Joash is not. He seems to

carry himself and be dressed as someone with money, a lot of money—and he looks awfully familiar…just don't recognize the name, I need his last name.

- Will he help his parents and these other people?
- Joash apparently has also become a Jesus guy or something like that. A new Christian maybe? Sounds like all the homeless group including his parents are Christians as well, interesting…
- Most interesting nugget—I heard the names Gideon and Marie. Are they talking about the Lars? How are they connected to the Lars?

Spencer stood from her seat, a lump rising to her throat. Moisture softly developed along dainty palms. Nerves—she had not dealt with nerves like these in the entirety of her quest as a journalist. The potential size of this story seemingly brought with it a weight of worry about not dropping a single note of it. *This is your opportunity, Spence. Do not let it go.*

She slowly approached the group, hiding her notebook and therefore any clue that screamed *reporter*. Once she made her way through the groups of folks all standing amid the diner to reach the main character, Joash, she let out an audible gasp. Closing in to this degree gave a far clearer view of this man. *Joe Lar.* The *Joe Lar. So that means…Gideon and Marie, were they distant relatives? Did they know about his parents? Was he a foster? Why was this hidden?*

"Ma'am? Ma'am? Are you all right? Do you need assistance?" Joe's voice broke the stunned trance.

"Hel—um, hello, yes, my sincere apologies. I just…"

Spencer was losing her mind in front of the man who reigned over her career in more ways than one. Not only was his family the owner of the only national newspaper and the largest local print company, but he was also now the center of what could be a world-changing story. And she had just been standing there in the middle of a crowd silently gawking at this stranger of a man, then stammered for a solid ten seconds.

"Hello, sir. My name is Spencer. My apologies for the confusion there—you just looked familiar to me for a moment. I think I was incorrect. I just couldn't help but overhear your story and would love to know more about such an inspiring tale. I am a hopeless romantic and am always intrigued by real-life dramas that bring such joy." Impressed and pleased with her ability to pull herself together, she ended her monologue with a professional albeit polite and timid grin in hopes of warming her audience.

"Oh, no worries, I get that often, honestly. Nice to meet you, Spencer."

Joe extended a greeting hand. *He bought it and ate it up.* Spencer reached her hand to his in response to his gesture. "Good to meet you as well. Joash, is it? May I sit?" Back in her comfort zone, she sat amid the group on an open stool without awaiting Joe's welcome. "So, I overheard correctly that these are your parents and you all have been separated your whole life until this year! That is so sad, but it is so wonderful that you found one another!" She allowed the words to sing with enthusiasm and wander as if she were a daydreaming daisy. *Keep up the innocent illusion; it's what got you here. As painful as it may be, play dumb.*

Joash let out a slight chuckle. *Quite fiery, this one.* "Yes, you heard correctly. We were separated nearly the moment I was out of the womb. Miraculously brought back together. Thankfully now we'll have the opportunity to grow as a family," Joash stated, pausing and awaiting the elegantly spritely woman to respond. He was nervous as he guessed where her questions might lead, and he feared diving too deep into the darkness that was the Lars.

"So how were you separated? I did not hear you mention that part of the story. You have everyone here on the edge of their seat, me included, I'm certain of it. Enlighten us—exactly how were you separated for so many years?"

That did not take long at all; this woman is...bold. "Ahh yes, it would be foolish of me to not assume someone would come up with such a question. Although currently we're not at liberty to discuss such details. There are other parties involved, and I would not feel like an honest man if I spoke of the entire ordeal publicly without discussing it with them first. There are unfinished portions to this *story*, as you say. It is still playing out. This is all brand new." Joash gave his response in his most political tone while still holding a polite smile, thus removing any premonition of hostility. *She is not pleased. Why would a stranger have such emotion over me stating I cannot share? Nosy one.*

"Entirely understandable. My apologies for prying, sir. You all have a good night. I hope someday I run into you all again and can hear the rest of your story. Truly, it is moving. Quite the *miracle*, as you say. Lovely to meet you all."

Spencer said her adieu quickly enough that no one could respond yet calmly enough to not alert any of them to her lack of care beyond getting this story. And *get it* she would. Time to make the trip back to the city. This was not the finished product she had promised her boss, yet she knew it packed enough promise to pardon her further delay. Spence slid out of the diner quietly, slipping also from Joe's line of sight.

"Well, she was sweet; quite the dreamer, it sounded like." Donna cooed over the young lady, not necessarily expecting a response.

"Yeah, she was interesting." The sentence rolled off Joe's lips, falling to a near whisper.

"Oh wow. George, do you see that?" Donna challenged in a drawn-out gasp.

"Why, yes. Yes, I do." George let out a laugh.

"See what exactly? I apologize, did I miss something?" Joe pressed in sincerity.

"Oh, son, you may be oblivious completely, but you like that woman. That is what I would classify as love at first sight," Donna stated, wrapping her arms around her husband's waist and giving him a gentle squeeze.

"The way you looked at her is the way your father looked at me when we first met. The moment he knew I was his wife," Donna added.

"Ha! Oh, you cannot be serious. I know I am maybe slightly less cynical now that I have come to the realization of Jesus, but I am far from being ready to like, let alone love, another human being. I assure you there was no intention other than basic human kindness and respect in *the way I looked at her*. Although if or when I do find anyone in this life, I do hope it is a love like what I have seen of yours thus far." Joash shook his head, picking up his cup to take his final sip. *Empty.* Suddenly realizing how utterly exhausted he was, he knew he would need to find a hotel soon; driving home was not going to happen in his state. "All right, so what is your guys' plan going forward? Forgive me for asking this, as I truly do not understand the makings of the lifestyle you all have been forced to live. Where would you normally sleep tonight?" Joe questioned.

"The bridge you were looking for us by has been our temporary home. It of course is not where we plan to remain, as we know that might scare others who may simply be out for a walk. At this time, we've simply not found any better option for shelter. We're truly hoping this move may pave the way for a few of us to attain work and maybe move on from this season of our lives. That will take time, we are aware, but we have a good feeling about this town, these people. If that feeling is wrong, we will simply move on to the next," George said.

Joash paused for a moment; looking up and away from the few closest to him, he realized how many of the folks there must have been from this town. People who had been listening and receiving from their stories. "Hey, everyone!" he called out while standing from his seat. "Any of you who live in this town, where is the nearest hotel?"

"Susie's Inn!" a voice chimed from a window seat. "It is the only bed-and-breakfast in town, and it is home to the world's best omelet, bacon, *and* pancakes. Though I may be biased—my mother is the cook," the woman continued as she came into view.

"Thank you!" Joe exclaimed. "That sounds absolutely delightful. Could we speak a bit further on details?" He gestured for them to step away from the crowd. As they exited the diner, he continued, "Listen, I know most people would turn me down for what I am about to inquire of you. You heard our story. What you haven't heard is that as we sat, speaking of all that has happened within our lives, I became aware of a task being placed on my heart. I want to help all of them. Not just my family, all of them. I would be delighted to start tonight. How much to host all of us at the inn?" The woman simply took a deep breath, rapidly blinking, attempting to take in the current task. "I am entirely good for whatever the cost may be. I can get it to you however you wish—cash, card, check, whatever is needed—" Joe was cut off by the woman waving her hand.

"Hold on, hold on, I apologize for hesitating; it has nothing to do with finances. This town is a beautiful little town and has blessed me for years with friendship and safety. But it has been a long time since anyone boldly spoke about Jesus the way you all have; it has been a long time since anyone shared a testimony or a miracle. My faith has most definitely taken a seat on the back burner, and I began to even forget about faith. Recently, while on a run, I felt a pull toward God. I honestly believe it was the sunrise that morning. There is a verse I used to quote daily: 'The heavens declare the glory of God; the firmament showeth His handiwork.' Psalm 19:1. Anyway, when I felt the pull, I asked for something I hadn't asked for since my adolescence. I asked for God to give this town, and me, a divine appointment. Something that would wake us up back to His glory. Sir, I want to invite all of you to stay at the inn free of charge."

Joash began to interrupt with an insistence that her offer was far too large a gift. Before air could escape his lungs, her hand was up, inclining him to halt his thoughts. *This woman and her hands.*

"Do not fight me on this, please. I couldn't care less how much money you have. Nor do I want you to decline my invitation out of false humility. Biblical humility allows you to receive blessings bestowed upon you regardless of whether you feel they are deserved. Beds, showers, meals on us; bring the entire group. The address is 117 Maple Lane. Walk out the diner to the main street here, take a right on Main, four blocks down take a left on Maple Lane, and we're five down on the right. I will see you soon; I am heading over first to prepare Ma."

Without another word, the woman was in her car backing out on her way to prepare. As he reentered the diner, a giddiness built in his chest. He could nearly skip. *Pansy*, he scoffed. *Yeah, Pansy and I do not give a rip. This is exciting.* He argued with himself. He approached the group, and they all paused, giving him analyzing brow raises. A man walking in with a grin that size had to have something up his sleeve.

"Hey, everyone, I have a surprise. I am going to need the full group to follow me." Joe gave a head nod to the employees and other townsfolk. "Good night, everyone. Thank you for the wonderful meal; tip is on the table. Hope you all have a blessed evening." He spun on his heels and headed toward the door, leaving his friends stunned and still unsure. Stopping at the door and turning to look at them all, he sensed their uncertainty. *Valid.* "Listen, I would tell you all what is planned. However, I would truly prefer it to remain a surprise. I ask you to trust me; I would never put you in any danger. I know that because of the family I was associated with, some of you are hesitant to believe me, but I assure you, you will not regret trusting me right now." He halted his breath in anticipation of their next move.

George stood. "Come on, you all, let's follow. I do not know what he has in store, but I trust him. I have peace about trusting him. You all can as well."

The group slowly stood to their feet, and a slight excitement began to rise to their cheeks beneath the anxiousness. As they filtered through the door and began their walk, Joash had to slow down on repeat, having a humorously difficult time suppressing his excitement to walk slowly enough for the entire group to keep with his stride.

Once they were in front of the inn, as Joash began to ascend the steps to the front door, a doubtful realization hit a few in the clan. Turning to face them all as the sound of walking diminished behind him, he simply smiled an assurance of comfort, tilting his head to direct them to come on in. As the group nervously entered, there stood what seemed to be the entire staff of the inn, with smiling faces. The place was lit with elegant light fixtures as well as candles that scented the air with lilac. The floors were cherry oak, and the trim along the doors and windows matched. The 1920s furniture, still gleaming like new, bore historic glamour.

"Welcome, everyone! Please, come in!" The woman standing in the center gestured, nearly grabbing them all by the hand and pulling them farther into the home. "My name is Sue," she stated, lifting her hand toward the sign hanging in the entryway: *Susie's Inn*. "But you can call me Ma. We have ten bedrooms, seven with two queens, three with one king. Each has its own restroom, television, coffee station, robes, and slippers. Please feel free to utilize those and enjoy the spacious showers. Just know to maybe save ten minutes between each shower for hot water and keep each shower to a max of fifteen minutes. My apologies that they cannot be longer with such a large group, but we hope that will suffice. We also have two dining rooms, the east wing dining hall for breakfast and the west wing for lunch and dinner. Breakfast is served from seven a.m. to ten thirty a.m., lunch from twelve to three thirty, and dinner from four thirty to eight.

"There is a wonderful garden out back, along with tennis and shuffleboard. In the basement, we have our pool hall with billiards, a library, and our little theater. That area is open until ten p.m. Please feel free to enjoy all the rooms at your leisure, and if you need anything at all, find any of our workers and we would be honored to assist you."

George cleared his throat, pulling himself from a trance. Leaving the rest of his family and friends behind in awe, he stepped forward, tapping his son on the shoulder. "Joe, this is... we can't. I mean, they can...but..." The words could not escape through the longing to cry, choked back.

"Dad, this is not a gift from me but from the inn. They are blessing all of us with a free stay, free meals, and free hospitality. All in exchange for the hope they received through hearing our story. I gathered from the insistence of this woman right here," he said, nodding toward Joanne, the daughter of the inn owner, "I dare not resist their invitation. It would not be biblical," he added with a wink. George stepped back, allowing a tear to slip, swallowing the urge to wholly sob.

Ornate beauty was woven throughout the design of all objects and structures throughout the inn. The majesty was not in the physical handiwork alone, though that in itself was breathtaking; the majority of the awe sewn into this structure came from the grace, humility, and sheer unconditional love pouring from the hearts of each staff member, generously bestowed upon George and all with him. It was a kindness he had, up until now, not received, making it semidifficult to grasp.

Donna did not say a word. However, as the emotions of her husband and all the other members of their group oozed out of them, the same passion flowed through her, and within moments her arms were flung around the owner and her daughter, embracing them both with gratitude of monumental proportions.

"It is our honor," Ma whispered. "Now dry your tears, pull yourself together, go find your rooms, and meet us in the morning for breakfast. Any allergies in the group?" Not a word was uttered as shock was still weaving its way through hearts and minds, bringing with it speechlessness. "Well, I will take silence as a no. You all have a good evening and a good rest!"

The inn crew dispersed and made way for their guests to venture up to their quarters. Years of bonding and building of friendships within the village had made it easy to determine room assignments. Gratitude born from years of filth made each person more than willing to keep showers under fifteen minutes. Murmurs of how wonderful the water felt and the scent of the soap filtered through the halls, followed by giggles of girls as they braided hair and laughs of men as they remembered what their faces looked like clean shaven. The inn had gone above and beyond with toiletries, linens, and even clothing they had gathered and washed over the years of folks visiting and leaving behind quality outfits.

Joe and George made their way down to the pool hall, laughing and overhearing the gratitude wander through the walls. "Dad, this needs to be just the beginning," Joash said, leaning against the table and sinking a solid.

"What do you mean, son?" George challenged, raising an eyebrow, revealing competitive impulses as his son pulled ahead in their game.

"I do not mean to sound as though I am using you or the village you have watched over; however, this could be the start of something grand. Imagine, we begin by having this hotel assist in a night of showers, clean clothes, and a nice meal. That alone perks up the faces and posture of these folks and fuels them with the confidence to nail any interview they can attain. Within days, they could have jobs. Imagine if there were a building funded by people who chose to assist that would practically be given away with no rent. Instead, once they have jobs, we could require payment be made to their own account in the form of rent, simply to renew their familiarity with paying bills consistently. Once the account reaches a substantial level of savings, we return it to them. At which point they would then be able to afford, at the very least, an average apartment. Their room would become available for the next in line in need. We would not be able to save the world, but we could save at least several. Imagine if it grew nationally, beyond several, then…"

George's expressions spoke bewilderment. Surreal—having the intense irrational reality of a dream, by *Webster's* definition. His long-lost son-turned-billionaire, demonized, having found his real family, had now chosen his real family over those that had given him everything he had. While also coming to know the Lord and being so immediately enthralled with the idea of becoming the Lord's vessel to the poor. *All praise be to you, Father. Thank you for sacrificing your son to save mine.*

DARING THE BOARD

"Blasted *codes*!" Vexation hissed an echo along the walls of Joash's apartment. Speed carried a binder of pages into the air, slowing as they dispersed among surrounding surfaces. Joash had never faced such turmoil when pursuing a build plan or neighborhood improvement in his years working under Gideon, the reason being that the people supporting the Lar family were most often self-fulfilling gluttons for glamour and prestigious allure, which was easy enough to give. Most often it never directly brought on political or societal issues that offended the Lars' flock of followers in the slightest. The people who supported the signatures for the codes required to begin building Joe's dream destination for the restoration of the homeless in the city were the same ones who had previously signed for spikes under bridges faster than the speed of light. His proposed plan was expected to receive backlash. Still, he had been confident enough in his pitch that there would be enough agreements to back his vision. Not a single "maybe." Every signature was preceded by absolute disgust-driven responses in email. That was the issue. He needed an in-person presentation.

He knew the power of presence, of face-to-face interaction. Especially now that he had the Alpha and Omega on his side. Zoning for commercial properties had been his forte, yet zoning for a project that not only lacked in fulfilling selfish desires of the community but also took from said community was a vastly different animal. Ringing interrupted his spiral into discouragement. Joash had barely mouthed the beginning of a hello before he heard, "Are you out of your damn mind!"

"Ahh, Brim! I was wondering when, or if, I would hear from you again! What is with the oh-so-*kind* greeting, brother?"

Brim was Joe's closest—and truthfully, only—friend from college. Joash knew eventually this call would come when Brim received word of his current less-than-Lar-material plans for the city. Though he retorted to Brim's tough-love greeting with seemingly confident humor, on the inside, the panic was settling in. As a man who could never approach life with emotion for fear of being viewed as a wuss, he had never before mentioned to even himself how vast an impact Brim had had on his life. This man meant the world. This man was his brother.

"Joe, listen, have you seen the papers? Forget even answering the question, just go grab the paper." There the hairs of his neck went again, standing on end. What had the press gotten ahold of? His whole story? How? He had always been wise enough to avoid any form of media he did not flat-out welcome. Obviously until now. His feet carried him to the door and down the stairs. Stocking feet. Brim holding silently on the other end of the line. He reached the lobby, making his way to the newsstand. The headline read "Lar Family Secrets Unleashed: Devastation for Elevation." Joash scanned the article: "The Lars—loved by many, feared by more. We all knew the golden family was raking in millions. Let's face it, we all also knew that the millions were gathered in less-than-lawful situations, but how dark do their deeds truly travel?" His gut grew sore; his lungs grew tighter. "As spoken by peers of Joe Lar himself, also known as Joash (the birth name given to him by his true parents), these deeds dive to depths of kidnapping, murder, and hateful oppression of any threat. Oppression that is powerful enough to drive said threats to homelessness."

His eyes jumped to the bottom of the page to see the author: *Spencer Jones*. "Spencer, Spencer Jones…Spencer." Joe's pupils dashed back and forth over the name as if reading Spencer Jones would spark memories of who this reporter was.

Brim shouted from the other end of their ongoing albeit forgotten phone call, "Joe! Joe! Blast it all, Joe!"

"Yeah, Brim, I'm here. Sorry, I'm here."

"Hell, man, is this all true, Joe? Did they really…is this true?"

Joash let out a sigh and took a look around him, realizing that everyone was watching him with their breath caught in their throats. He spun gracefully on his heels and began a stoic walk back toward the stairs, ignoring their gazes.

"Yeah, yeah, Brim, it's true. It's honestly written well, from what I skimmed, though I never expected, nor wished in any capacity, that it would be announced to the world like this. I

guess I never pictured it being announced to the world at all."
Joe's voice began to trail off as he entered his apartment and sat
on his sofa, placing the phone on speaker and tossing it on the
coffee table.

"Wow, Joe, wow. This is why I haven't seen you at all for
nearly three years? Where have you really been? Yeah, know
what, scratch that; do not answer that. Meet me at Howard's.
I'm buying you a beer, maybe bourbon. We'll talk about it then."

Joash had no opportunity to respond before the other end of
the line went silent. He did not want to leave at the moment, yet
he needed to meet with Brim; his spirit needed a familiar friend.
He pulled a hoodie on and slapped a baseball cap over his tou-
sled hair, creating a poor excuse for a disguise. Wallet and keys
slid off the counter, quickly, into a pocket. White knuckles still
clutched the newspaper. He headed out to trot over to Howard's.
One measly little block. Walking would be his best option; perhaps he could meekly slip unnoticed into the bustling New York
crowd. *Doubtful.* The moment his feet hit the lobby floor, he
sensed eyes on him again, or was it merely paranoia? Pushing
through the doors, Joe was hit with the first flash.

"Joe Lar, what do you have to say about the headlines? Are
they true?"

"Joe, what will this mean for the Lar family? Are you claiming them? Will you sue?"

The questions dived at him as if they were angry wasps hungry for violence, out for blood. *In Jesus's name. In Jesus's name.*
Joe's heart was proclaiming the only name he knew to call on at
this moment. Before the past few months, he would have simply

slipped them a finger, threatened to sue *them*, and pushed violently through the man-eating mass. This time he felt as though all he needed to do was call on the name of the Lord, whom he had now begun to seek daily. It worked, somehow; he found himself running past the line, and not a single camera followed. *Thank you, Lord.* The last time he had felt such a deep agony in his gut was the day he first met his real father, finding out the truth about his life. He had hoped to heal and grieve far longer than this before experiencing anything close to such despair. At least this time he had Him. He had Jesus.

Joash pushed through the bar doors, his focus finding Brim quickly. *Thank God he's already here.* Brim was tucked back into a corner booth, wisely hidden from the eyes in the restaurant. Joe took his seat, and as his voice rose to speak, the walls of his throat began to thicken, choking any sound from escaping.

"Joe, take a breath, take a drink. Do you still drink? The article mentioned changes you've been through lately; not sure how to navigate this territory. Truthfully, you do not even look like the same Joe. You do look more like a Joash. As though the structure of your face profoundly changed somehow."

Joash could not help but beam with gratitude for the confirmation of the change the Lord had begun in him. "Well, Brim, I am still navigating this all. I do know this, I will not ever drink as the Joe you used to know drank. I lost time, friends, and life because fof the nightly visits with near alcohol poisoning. I honestly moved on from that *before* I found..." He paused. His breath hitched yet again; his gaze ripped away from his brother.

Fear swept over him as images of possible reactions to his claimed faith, in the form of judgment and ridicule from his long-time confidant, coursed through his nerves. "Jesus?" Brim's suggestion brought with it comfort and sincere acceptance, allowing Joash to release the tension that had gripped nearly every muscle.

"Yes, truthfully. I know you may find it amusing to see Joe Lar claiming to have been redeemed. Part of my mind still scoffs at the idea now and then. But then I set my thoughts on Him, and immediately my salvation makes sense again. Without even a word spoken. It has been an adventure, to say the least. One that I fear is about to become much darker than I believe I am prepared for. What will happen to this city?" Joe's voice fizzled to a dull whisper.

Brim solidly gripped the glass in front of him, gulping the rust-colored liquid swiftly as though it were air. "Who is this Spencer Jones? I've yet to hear this name, and unfortunately, I have become familiar with most journalists worthy of any front page, even a small publication such as this. Seems odd to have an unknown writer cover such a damning story."

Brim posed the question while reaching into the satchel that hung along his side, pulling out from it the blasted paper and tossing it into the center of the table. The men sat staring in silence at the now-wrinkled paper. The words began to blur as they held their long gaze. Both of their minds boiled, rolling the name around in their throats, searching for hidden knowledge in their subconscious. Eventually reaching a point of disconnection, zoning into numbness. Joash sipped slowly, in the back of his mind asking the Lord to reveal this person and, once she was revealed, to give him the words or actions needed to address her. Praying in his thoughts was slowly becoming normal, though so was remaining too numb at times to hear the Father's response or instruction. He'd need to work on that.

"Spence! Hey, sweet girl. It's been too long! Where have you been?" A jolly voice from behind the bar rolled through the crowd toward the door. Having just entered, a young woman strode toward the stools near her greeter. Bodies blocked Joash and Brim's vision. They held out, staring, waiting for a peek of their possible culprit. As the crowd cleared and made a path, Joash's eyes met the face belonging to the nickname, the shock causing his grip to tighten, shattering the glass amid his palm. The woman's eyes darted over to witness the commotion; upon seeing the face of her victim, she snatched her bag from the bar and sprinted back toward the exit.

Joash didn't hesitate, standing and chasing after her, leaving Brim behind to apologize to the angered bouncers coming to manage the shards of glass. "Spencer Jones! I do not believe you have the right to be walking away from me right now. Not the way of a solid seasoned journalist brave enough to release this piece of art." Joe had just realized he had grabbed the paper, as he was holding it up at her. This was the first time he has felt true anger and betrayal since the last time he saw the Lars.

It had been three months with nearly no anger. Staring at this woman who seemed so innocent but had attempted to tear apart his name had his blood boiling over. She had stopped cold when she heard her name bellow out from the fury-ridden chest behind her. She stood, facing away from him, clutching the strap of her bag as if it were her savior. Joash stood still, his hand still extended. As if waking from a dream, he began to open his eyes to the realization that his stance was accusatory, demeaning. The stance he had used for years to induce fear. "I apologize for coming off so rudely. I swear I do not truly have any ill intent against you. All I ask is an hour of your time, at most. I would simply like to discuss what you wrote. We can discuss it here. In public, no tricks. Please, Spencer." He stood silent, lowering his arm and awaiting any response from the frozen woman in front of him. She could feel his hand lower, though it did not cause the bumps lining her skin to follow. They remained raised, announcing that she continued to be on high alert.

As though stuck in a bed of molasses, she felt as though she could not move enough to take a breath, let alone turn to face the man whose life was now permanently scarred because of her. "This is what it will take for anyone to treat you with an ounce of respect in this field." If her boss's words were true, why did she feel as though this had sunk her farther to the bottom of the barrel rather than raising her to the mountaintop? Hours came and went before she made her decision to face Joash. *Fire of God.* She did not *not* believe in God. She simply had no desire to trust anyone aside from herself with her life. Still, the name made her spirit aware of the possibility that this man might indeed genuinely know the Creator of the world, if He did exist. Connecting with bright glaciers that lined the irises under his stern brows, Spence sensed the arctic gaze submerging her further, although, beneath the initial sharpness of his stare, there lingered a heat, a warmth, a passion.

Gather your senses. Absolutely not—this is not the time, Spencer. Get it out of your head. The lecture cleared the thoughts of attraction from her line of sight, though they very clearly tucked themselves into her core memory and subconscious, planning to eventually revisit her. Her stubbornness to remain poised and unaffected forced her to speak; she was unwilling to appear weakened by his presence. "I can agree to that. I can agree to give you time to discuss whatever it is that will bring you closure, Joe. Just do not tell me I owe you anything. I *owe* no one. However, I can understand that it would be kind of me to give you answers." The elastic muscles of her vocal folds remained calm compared to their typical nervous shaking—good. She gestured for him to take the lead back to the bar. "After you, miss." His words were polite, his intention to keep her in his sight not as well hidden as he had intended. Regardless, she led the way.

She walked with a boldness that she had pretended to have her entire life. Perhaps one day said boldness would envelop her, fill her, be her. As they made their way past the bar, the bartender shot them both a puzzled look, followed by a raised eyebrow at Spence, ensuring she was safe. A nod in counter assured all was fine. *Somehow* discernment revealed in the subconscious that safety was a nonissue. They settled into a back booth, both ordering water. He ordered a basket of onion rings. *Hmm, he feels comfortable enough to eat. Strange for a man who was seemingly in such distress when he chased after me. He's unique…not cocky but confident in his choices. Of course, this is Joe Lar.* The hair that lay in strands over the left side of his forehead framed the shape of his expression. *He's studying me.* Immediately beads of sweat coated her palms. Before allowing silent inquisition a permanent grasp on her attention, Spencer took power in words.

"What exactly are you looking to discuss, Mr. Lar?" She spoke, exuding instruction rather than inquiry. The look that took over Joe's face confirmed it. It was as if he recognized it was now he who held the responsibility of another's demands.

It was now he on the podium being prodded yet again, rather than his intended questioning of Spencer as the culprit on the stand. *I cannot believe this is working.* Her face remained stoic, not revealing her disbelief, which whispered below the surface. "I would ask why you wrote what you wrote. I would ask why you would put such a dangerous story out, knowing the lives it could destroy. However, I am assuming this is your first hit of a story with enough gusto to finally place you on the map as a journalist. I can respect the drive to reach your goal. Another assumption is that it has been a goal for a large portion of your life. I do not want to waste time asking why. Rather, I would like to know, do you understand the gravity of the consequences this city may now face?"

Spencer stared blankly at this man before her. Was he threatening her? She remained silent, attempting to dissect his point thoroughly before offering her answer.

"Whoa, before you go there, Ms. Jones, my statement was not a threat. I would never threaten you. Simply a question as to whether you are aware of what those who inhabit New York are capable of."

Hesitating, she defended herself. "Of course, Mr. Lar." She used the name again, noticing his flinch as the title left her lips. Power play. "Of course, I know what the people of New York are capable of. I have witnessed the strength of those around us throughout my entire life. I am a New Yorker; I know what I am capable of. We are a strong people."

Joe shook his head in response. "No, Ms. Jones, you still do not understand: 1971, the riots of Fifth Street; 2005, the riots over the Brooklyn Bridge being threatened with replacement; 2010, one of the largest and most prestigious law firms was taken down by *the people* over a comment made in bad taste. Now you tell the people of New York that the Lars, whom the rich love and feed off of and whom the poor envy and nearly worship, are murderous, kidnapping, cheating, conniving criminals, and you expect what? Peace and love?" Joash paused for a moment. Spencer was stunned silent at this point. She truly had not thought of the possibility of *the people* reacting to the news in violence.

She had expected the Lars to be shunned, maybe even run out of town by their colleagues, and, of course, possibly put in prison. However, all of that felt correct: they deserved punishment, and the city and Joe deserved justice. What if she had also opened a Pandora's box of anger and entitlement, causing a war to spill out into the streets and businesses of her city? The thought made her slink back in her chair a bit, no longer standing proud.

"Listen, Spence—that's what they call you, right? Spence, I do not want to belittle you; that is not why I want to talk. I do have an unrealistic hope that somehow this is a quite vivid dream, that I will wake up shortly and this paper will have been part of a nightmare. Unfortunately, I know that is truly not the case. I let my guard down that night at the diner. I cannot be angry with you over this—I was not acting responsibly. I allowed my excitement to get the best of me." Joe paused, challenging himself as to what he was truthfully expecting from this discussion.

As if a light bulb were actually hovering above his head, his countenance lit immediately, announcing an idea had been bestowed upon him. "I know what I would like to ask. Not only would it advance your career as a journalist, but it would also help me to better the city and possibly halt any and all backlash, at least in the form of riots. We may receive backlash in politics from those with stock in keeping the city 'clean of the homeless,' but that will also be demolished if you help me. I want you to write about the project I am working on. Announce it to the city and announce the rejection I am receiving from the board." Joe took a breath and held it still until he received a response from the woman now staring at him in pure judgment. *This man is outrageous.*

"Slow down, please, *Joe.* What project? Why is the board saying no? You understand that if I write against this so-called board my job would be at their disposal. There are people who have enough power to ensure I never publish another piece again. You of all people should recall that this is a frequent response from those in positions of power."

Ouch. The painful refining of truth. Joe swiftly began to reminisce on the positions he had removed from the companies of those who had stood in his way. No longer yielding the desire to utilize these *abilities* he was raised with posed a problem. He found irony in the fact that he had wasted his years of cruelty on those who were the exact opposite of the men and women who should have been reaping immense amounts of cruelty themselves. Rapaciousness bled onto innocent folks who were barely scratching out a living to stay afloat, simply doing their jobs, or staying true to honesty and integrity. Rather than standing up to those filled with pure corruption. *I am forgiven.* He had lost count of the frequency with which this phrase had fallen off his lips or swirled about in his mind over the past few months. Forgiving others, while it could be a daunting task, held no comparison to the struggle of receiving and accepting forgiveness for oneself. The words still felt empty. Hope still lay in his ribs, whispering the thought that one day, he would say it and mean it. He met her eyes again.

"You are correct. I have made decisions to run over someone's life when they stepped their foot into my territory, blocking my path. Therein lies devastating regrets. I do not anticipate acceptance of the changes that I have endured to become a far different man. However, if you do choose to see who I am now, you may become aware that the goals I have currently are to love and help the lives I have inflicted. I want to turn an abandoned area into a full city for those who are without a home. One that not only provides a roof over their heads but significant resources to rehabilitate them, to give them lives again."

Spencer was unable to contain the imminent explosion of interest bursting from her once-slouched shoulders now upright, bringing her head near the ceiling, exuding through her eyes a sudden brightness. All resistance had diminished as she had been gifted with writing a piece carrying the potential to inspire the creation of a sanctuary for those who had lost any form of serenity and peace. Her immediate shift in nature overrode the need to pose questions as to why the casualty of her most recent production had chosen to present her with opportunity rather than strip her of her dreams.

Her overabundance of passion-driven shock was followed by his lack thereof, evident in equal measure. It was as though he had anticipated such a reaction from the reporter and was unfazed. As if he had her pegged. Rather than allow this to dim her drive to see such a gift through, she allowed herself to regain composure, choosing to offer bold acceptance along with a challenge in response. "I do not care what your game is. If you indeed have a scheme behind requesting my help, I pay no mind to it. I will not dull a hunger to encourage a movement that betters this city simply because of a feeble attempt to intimidate me. I will have you know, you may believe you know me, but I assure you, Joash, you do not. What you may have guessed correctly is that I would never refuse an opportunity to pour life into those who inhabit the same streets as I do. So, I can begin writing the moment I get back home tonight. What I need from you is details. Every detail you can possibly provide. My first question is simply this: What is in it for you?"

Joash sat straight and held out a hand. "All I want is to begin to do right by this city after years of doing wrong. To begin attaining such aspirations, I must invite *the people* to lead my project, as they rightfully should. That is the only hammer that will inspire the board to budge. Once we budge them, we move them. Once we move them, we change them. Once we change them, we change the lives of those they are currently standing on."

Conversation flowed as the two contemplated the trust they were able to bestow on the other, as well as the consequences, good and bad, of the plan laid out before them. Bodies swept by in and out of the tavern. Their surroundings both grew in volume and dulled to a whisper as the hours came to a close, leaving them alone with the rookie behind the bar and the veteran in front of it. They heard the calls of the owner as he peeked around the corner, singing a familiar classic. Though it indicated that they did not need to head to their dwelling, home was where they were headed. A handshake and admitted nervousness parted the two. They would meet again at dawn, when an article would be released in pursuit of transforming the Big Apple—so long as the pair had not bitten off more of the Golden Delicious than they were able to chew.

PRAYING THE PRAYERS

Swift feet, revolving glass, down the stairs to the sidewalk, nearly falling into the street. Her intuition of traffic's obscene capabilities to remove her from this life thankfully brought her to a halt preceding disaster. Spencer was all but hyperventilating; her chest heaved each breath with despair, with immediate regret. Metal on rubber whipped past her in blurs, sweeping her baby hairs across her forehead. The street spun. A grasp on her shoulder—hardy, sturdy, safe—caused her lungs to slow. Adjusting her to face him, he offered comfort as she met his eyes, allowing him to see her fear.

"Joash, what did we just do? There are cameras. I know your *family* runs this; however, we do not have any idea where you sit with the Lars at this moment. For all we know, they could have a hit out on you for allowing their horrific truth to buzz through the city they've practically run for so many years, along with the rest of the US. My assumption is that is not a small hindrance to them, and from the sounds of it, they have ended people for less. Now I am an accomplice. We just sent a suicide attempt out through the printers. If it's not my actual life, they'll at least end my professional one. We must undo it. We must take this back."

Joash gripped his hands around Spencer's shoulders, guiding her to stop in her tracks. A terror-plastered expression shone out of her eyes, her furrowed brow, her frown. "Listen, I know you are afraid, Spence. I understand entirely the risk you chose to partake in and, in doing so, the possible fate you accepted. Feeling afraid, unsure, and unsteady is entirely valid within the confines of this decision we are implementing. You are a grown woman; I do not have any intent to force your hand, nor do I fancy manipulating you. Maybe I would have not batted a lash at it in the past. However, I now want no part in forcing anyone to do anything. You are free beyond a shadow of a doubt to go back in there and turn me in or do whatever you feel you must to remove yourself from the situation. All I am asking is that you ponder the two separate choices calmly and precisely to ensure you have a clear understanding of the choice before you. Choosing to end this or choosing to attempt to change a small part of the world."

As though she had been mastering the act from childhood, Spencer pulled herself together. With a wipe of her eyes, a brushing back of dark strands, and a straightening of her clothes, there was no sign that a mere second ago she was riddled with distress and panic. "I want to meet them. Take me to meet them." Insistence and courage brought forth a woman's demand that no man could refuse. There was power in Spencer. Joash could see it, like a phoenix in her eyes. Yearning beat within his chest to fly alongside her without end in sight, though admitting such adoration and admiration to even himself felt immeasurably daunting. The two rode in silence for a while; no longer needing a GPS to guide him to the inn, Joash chose to break the silence with song. He had not dared to press Spence about where her faith was, if she had one. Up to this point, it seemed irrelevant to their situation, and he had not felt any sort of prompting to mention such things. Aside from a mention of his prayers to make this happen and his trust in God that it would.

He hadn't spoken about God to draw any attention to or from Spencer; it was merely natural for him to speak, as it was true. He thought about it at this moment, scrolling through the worship songs he had flooded his phone with shortly after his father warned him, "You must be watchful of what your ears and eyes receive and what your mouth speaks; if you genuinely want to grow closer to Jesus, there is a lot that can distract you from him, biblically 'sinful' or not." His hand hovered, nervous to choose.

"Joe, if I may be so bold, you're driving—give me the phone," Spence sassed, simultaneously swiping the device from his palm. Joash held his breath as she scrolled, anxiously unsure what this woman's response might be. *Why is her opinion having such a hold on you?* He shook the question loose, focusing his eyes on the road and his mind on slowing the pounding pulse he swore had become audible. Her thumb slowed to a stop. Tap, tap again, tap once more. Her other hand reached for the volume in the car, turning it to an impressive number.

She sat back and stared straight ahead; her focus returned to their destination as she locked her eyes on the pavement, swallowed at a steady speed of sixty-five. Instrumentals began to sound from the speakers in his car.

> Peace, bring it all to peace
> The storm surrounding me
> Let it break at Your name
>
> Still, call the sea to still
> The rage in me to still
> Every wave at Your name
>
> Jesus, Jesus, You make the darkness tremble
> Jesus, Jesus, You silence fear

Faint glimmers caught his peripheral gaze—tears falling gently, silently, down flushed cheeks. A panic grew within his core. Was she upset? Was she hurt? Was she afraid? The multitude of questions stirred worry, causing him to reach toward the phone in rescue mode, having allowed himself to agree with the fear-spoken intrusive thoughts. Her hand grasped his, halting his attempt. Her hand stayed. *I have her in my sight; I always have. She needs this. You can entrust her to me.* Joash recognized the still, small voice with less hesitation each time He spoke. In his quiet place, he confirmed back, *I trust you, Father. If you require anything of me to help her walk through this, help me to obey, and help me to renounce the lie of fear immediately each time it rises.*

His tension released, and his stomach settled. He listened to the words, the music, the sound of her silence as she received the movement of the Holy Spirit. His hand stayed put. When the song ended, silence made its notice and remained for the duration of the ride. It was a heavy silence, a comfortable heavy. A warm quilt wrapped around the two, as though rather than riding in a moving vehicle, they were parked on a sofa, fireplace roaring. Serenity rode the waves of the air, its thickness nearly visible. Neither of them made eye contact, and they continued to peer straight toward the destination. Still, two smiles formed in cohesive agreement of joy. Spence had promised herself that she would never allow another human being to initiate her pursuit of faith. If she pursued any type of belief, she would do it on her terms, with no outside influence. That said, she had a hefty lack of explanation as to why she'd allowed herself to choose a song from the God category, nor could she verbalize the tranquility that had invaded her soul just now. She was a sheep, standing lost, alone, having been lured out of her flock by the world. But there He stood, off in the distance, heading her way, and all she longed for was to run and meet her Shepherd.

Invaded. No, she had invited this, and *something* had responded. Ideas of an almighty Creator who gave her life and more so *loved her* may have been the tools pulling at her cheeks. Stifling that thought as much as she could, she thought, *We cannot get ahead of ourselves here—it was just a song. Let's not decide our life's path with a song.* Was it? Was it just a song?

As the vehicle slowed to a stop, Spence opened her eyes. Vision blurred to awareness—sleep must have lured her eyelids closed. Head resting against the window, knees curled to chest, feet on the dash. When had she taken her shoes off? When had she drooled this much in her sleep? Attempting to keep her saliva a secret, she pulled her arms to stretch, casually sitting straight, slipping a sleeve against her cheek and resting her arm over the small puddle on the door. The inn stood in front of her and within it, a group of people she longed to meet. Sure, she had seen them before, but at that point she was out for a story. Here, she stood for their well-being. Nerves began to stir as what-ifs swung into thought. *What if—what if they do not forgive me?*

"They will not hold anything against you, especially if I do not, which is the case. They will trust you. You are trustworthy." Joash flashed a most sincere "trust me" smile. *How does he know what I feel constantly?*

"You pick your nails when you're nervous, you feel guilty about the original paper, and you care whether or not others trust you." *There he goes again. This man must be sent from God.* An intended joke riding inner thoughts startled awareness to the concept's possible, nay, probable truth. "Spencer, do you feel ready to face them now? I will not have you facing them feeling unprepared, unready, or anything less than at peace and ease prior to going in. We do not need to fuel any form of anxiety for you or them. There is no need to be anxious, though I am aware emotions do not tend to be rational often. Please, be honest, are you ready?"

His words seemed to calm her instantly. Had any man attempted to speak this way to her in the past, she would have smacked him, entered the inn, and faced the group head-on even while remaining unready. It was sheer sincerity that lined his voice, a sincerity that blossomed with trust rooted at its core.

"I should take five minutes, five minutes of silence, just sitting here in the car, and I will be ready. I've already begun to calm. Thank you."

She sat with her head back against the seat, her lids closed, and silently she prayed. *I am unsure how to begin, I guess. I know to address you as Father in Heaven…Father in Heaven, please help me walk into this inn. Please help me help them. Please ease this fear. I know it's a lot to ask for someone who has not spoken to you since I was a girl. Nonetheless, I ask. Amen.*

Spence had a talent she chose to utilize today; she had faced times prior when life was calling for her to rip off the Band-Aid. As if there were a tiny crew of miniature workers within the bowels of her soul whom she instructed *full speed ahead*, initiating them to shovel coals into the furnace that was her willpower, she fueled her adrenaline-burning ambition. Such a talent allowed her to grip the door handle and find her stance as she stepped out of the vehicle into the fresh air with no further hesitation. An instant leap. It allowed not a single deterrent to interrupt from the moment she emerged from the car to the rapping of her knuckles against the inn door. Rapping she was as Joash caught up, having been left in her smoke.

Her awareness rebounded as the door swung open, revealing two smiling faces, a large embrace, and finally, greetings of "Hello, you two! So glad you could finally make it! It is such an honor to meet you, Spencer. Please, come in, come in—we want to hear all about this proposed plan our son has been so secretive about!"

Question answered in a moment. There was not an ounce of insincerity lining the greeting. She was forgiven. Molecules of strength—every one being utilized to contain her tears of joy and to lift her arms in response to the hug. An embrace that embodied a toasty home on a crisp fall morning. She wanted to never release herself from it. Eventually, she regained her composure and settled from the high, by which time they had found themselves seated in the living room being served coffee while others drank a bit of tea instead. Joash could have extinguished a fire utilizing solely the sweat that coated his palms.

Nerves fired through his system at a significantly higher frequency than when he had contacted the board, even higher than when he had watched Spencer waltz into the building to publish her paper. As the heat of the coffee steamed his glasses, he sighed. Removing them to apply a quick swipe with the end of his T-shirt, he said, "We have been secretive about this plan, as it will draw significant attention to all of you. I have discussed this with my father, Spencer, and no one else. Even my father does not know the full extent of it, nor does he know what is about to happen in the streets of New York." Furrowed lines formed in the skin, alluding to a covert concern nestled within each redemption prospect. "Spencer and I met back up the evening after the Lars' names were plastered all over the newspapers. Originally, I had planned to give her a significantly aggressive verbal lashing and honestly to nearly threaten her career and mean it. I was seeing red when I saw her, when it clicked exactly who she was. However, though my temper still needs mounds of work, a holy man I have recently met redirected my thoughts and intentions and instead placed empathy and a new idea on my heart as to how she could repay me."

Joash paused, giving Spence a side-eye smirk, advising that his statement was mostly a jest. "And most importantly, we could make a true difference and change in this city. One that would laugh in the face of those who mock those financially smaller. It would, in turn, shed light on the truth that they are morally smaller instead. And having been one of them just months ago, I feel the need to take responsibility for their actions and make a change on behalf of all those like me. It is the absolute least I can do."

Windswept dirt skated the grounds. Tree limbs bent and whistled, submitting to blistered gusts. The world spun as normal while words were spoken, shared, questioned, and formed. The conversation lasted well into the night. It had begun with excitement, curiosity, fervor, followed by stages of confusion, gut-wrenching worry, and doubt. Ending in peace, hope, acceptance, and belief. The entirety of the group, two vigilantes not excluded, headed to bed most decidedly unable to truly sleep. Riddled with anticipation for the morning when New York City would be turned on its head. Rays swayed against the crisp blue vault, landing for a moment upon closed eyelids that had unknowingly found rest around 2:00 a.m.

It was now only 7:30 a.m., and Joash had his qualms about being forced awake by daylight. Nonetheless, the sour response was quickly removed by sheer boyhood excitement and mild anxiousness as he thought about the inner-city war he and his colleague were about to initiate. The clinking of dishes and murmurs of conversation pulled him upright, and the smell of bacon carried him across the floor. He was eager to head downstairs. As he turned in to the hallway, his hurried steps slowed. The heart-swelling picture now in his sight, one that had come into view as he rounded the corner into a dimly lit hallway, was that of a woman in a kitchen, engulfed in the same rays that had awoken him. The strands of her hair fell perfectly. Her eyelashes closed gracefully as she let out a laugh in response to something his mother had uttered. He could not even hear what. All his ears received was her laughter. All else was drowned. She stood with hip leaned against the counter, drying a dish his mom had just cleaned. For a moment they were at his mother's and father's home, visiting for a holiday, their children running amok and "Grandpa" letting it happen. Joe's face turned sour; his being accepted by the Lord remained a struggle to believe even still. And the Lord accepted everyone.

He would not allow himself to fantasize around the laughable notion that a woman, especially this woman, would even look in his direction as a mate. He still doubted he wouldn't fail at his walk in faith; he had been resting on today's excitement. Though, what about when it was all over? When they had the approval to build, when the homes and donation centers were built and as many homeless as possible had had their lives renewed and restored, then what? He'd most likely write that off as his one good deed of a lifetime and find his way back to alcohol, to loneliness—he'd fail God. He'd fail everyone. Perhaps that was why he needed so desperately for this to unfold.

"Get in here, Joash. The staring is getting to be awkward now."

Blasted... Joash thought. "Thank you for announcing that, Mother. You know how to embarrass me already. Must be an instinct for all moms, I suspect." He grumbled his jest as he made his way into the kitchen and seated himself at the opposite countertop.

"Oh, son, you do not know how long I've waited to embarrass you in front of a woman. It's what made me want a son from the very start." The two women laughed once more, though it did not hide the blush that arose across Spencer's delicate cheeks. Joash felt as though it also could not have stifled the heartbeat that increased in response to her blushing. She was perfection, inside and out. Though he'd choke himself in hopes of taking said opinion to his grave. If there was a man out there who deserved her love, he was certainly not it.

"Mr. Lar—Joash, I mean—it may interest you to look out to the front yard." Mousy vocals uttered by one of the inn workers pulled his curiosity. Turning to see the entire group of his father's family, he recognized the ever-so-subtle emotion that lay in their eyes. Fear. Not so simple—this was curious fear.

He strode over to the window with a silent demand to know the cause behind the sudden thickness possessing the air of the inn. "Careful!" A shouted whisper halted Joe. He moved to the side of a chair placed in front of the window and slid open the drapery just enough to peer out without demanding attention from whatever lay in wait on the lawn. There they were, in all their glory, cameras at the ready, devices already recording. The news must have been televised, allowing for Maywood natives to spread word of their town's newest inhabitants or for a bloodthirsty journalist to drag it out of Gideon and Marie.

"Turn on the news!" Joash demanded. With the channel pulled up in seconds, his surroundings went silent aside from the televised words. "Papers printed over the past week have unleashed secrets of immeasurable proportions. A story that New York has not seen in decades. The Lar family, one we all look up to and fear, may be far more dangerous than any of us could have imagined. Their son, Joe Lar, was in fact kidnapped as a child and raised as their own, due to Marie Lar's infertility issues. To keep their secret, the criminal couple forced Joe's family to live on the streets and promised they'd be allowed to live in return for their silence.

"Now that Joash, as he goes by these days, has come to know the truth, he has found his birth parents and is fighting to create a better life for them and all of New York's homeless population. However, it appears our city leaders would rather see our people suffer and want to strip them of their voice and right to seek a better life. Will this paper move the city to allow Joe Lar to make the largest change for our homeless population in history? Or will the voice of the government be too loud? More to come tonight on the Channel 7 six o'clock news."

RESTORING THE DEAD

The perfume of ripened apples was carried upon a chilled breeze and danced beneath his nostrils as Joash stepped through the front door. A mere shake of serene autumn peace interrupted by vocal bombardment paired less than admirably with nigh seizure-inducing flashing cameras. *I suppose that is one gratitude I owe to being a Lar. The capability to manage the vultures.* The bitter thanks to his name came and went as Joash stood his ground and controlled the mob. With a bellowing whistle and a raised hand, the crew fell close to silent, with only the occasional click of a photo being shot to break the silence.

"Thank you all for recognizing and responding to my request to turn this from a media mosh pit into a civil interview. I'm unsure how you all determined our location; however, I have begun to slowly understand what people mean when they state that everything has a purpose. So I do not believe you all being here is a mistake or an accident."

He was interrupted by the first question. "What do you mean by that, Joash? What has changed that has caused you to believe that statement?"

For a moment he felt fraudulent. That thought tended to crawl into the folds of gray matter from time to time, though it spoke loudest now. As he was standing in front of the media.

He had no more than a couple years ago stood in front of the same media as Joe Lar, heir to the metaphorical throne, reigning above New York City, above the country. Evil, crooked, a destroyer. Was he truly standing before them now as a man who had lost his worldly identity and been found anew in Christ Jesus? As Joash, a man boldly in pursuit of the fire of God? Was he real, or was this a facade, a mask to stuff the darkness behind, a darkness that would eventually seep through the straps around his head, the straps that held the mask in place? Was this his feeble attempt at diminishing the wrong he'd done by playing the "good guy" for a bit to ease a narcissistic personality that could not bear to be seen as wrong? The term "baby Christian," or "new Christian," was one he struggled with. It made him feel rickety, his feet attempting to remain in place atop the buoy tossed about the sea of unease and uncertainty. Thickened sweat moistened his face and palms, bringing the sense of capsizing to life.

As he sank into disconnection from reality, Joash was able to utter a prayer that most misunderstand or degrade the power of. *Help me, Father.* Zoe love was the definition of earth's Creator, the one who currently breathed life into the lungs of a man desperate for direction, the reason for the God of all, Lord of Hosts, to send his armies for Joash the moment he uttered the three words of prayer. In an instant Joash was lit from his spirit with understanding and an awareness of the Father's real presence. It was as though Jesus had stepped down from Heaven once more to stand aside and shepherd his sheep. Though Joash knew the Lord was not able to be seen with his eyes, he hoped the presence of the King of Kings would become irrefutable at that moment. So much so that there was an even more powerful hush over the crowd in front of him, as well as his family standing behind him.

Then came the words from his lips, as though the spirit of the Lord spoke through him. It was not a strange puppetry aura. Rather, it was as if the words Joash needed were being laid on his heart and the courage to speak them had been bestowed. "You all recognize me as a man that this city has loved, envied, feared, and even despised, though you would not have the gall to say so. Though they would have every right to have such opinions about me, as well as the rest of the Lar family. The things we have all done to climb to the position of power we hold now— or held—are unarguably atrocious. I recall one gentleman who worked as my assistant whom I made cry every day until he quit and ended up admitting himself for psychiatric help. I am sure you all remember that article. And to 'fix' that mistake, all our family did was throw money at it to alter the view of the public. If we looked like the hero, who cared if we were, in truth, the villain."

Joash paused a moment, then motioned for George to step forward with him. George removed his hat and shyly took his place aside his son. "Up until the day I met this man, I had no desire to change the monster I was. I was fueled by power, hate, anger, and a desire to harm to make myself feel superior. And no one could stop me. Yet this man stepped into our home and was brave enough to face all of us at once to bring the truth and to fight for others above himself. It is true, this man is my father. While I will be candid with details of how I was removed from his and my mother's care, I will state that the knowledge of my false identity caused me to lose myself entirely." The strong will fight a war to hold hostage one public tear; Joash choked back a sob and continued. "I searched for myself. I searched in every liquor bottle, in every pile of cocaine, in women, in self-harm, in meditation, in therapy, and eventually back to the alcohol, as it was the only substance through which I seemingly had the power to cause my pain to disappear. I could reach a specific moment in which every part of my life *seemed* to be *right*.

"We all have one substance that works best to veil the darkness, that provides the feeling of safety. However, I came to find shortly after an encounter with a man at a bar that the feeling of safety that any of those outlets provided was truthfully placing me in more danger than simply walking with the darkness, aware of it. Because you see, the feeling of safety when you are numbing your awareness to darkness is not providing you safety; it is removing your ability to see that you are walking hand in hand with what is aiming to kill you."

Joash paused; the words rolled through the folds of his brain and around the beat of his heart, eventually finding their way to his lips. As he spoke them, he heard his dad's voice, just as he had on April 13, 2014.

"'Turn your eyes to your Father in Heaven with surrender. You need Him, and He is simply awaiting your realization of that truth. *Come to Me, all who are weary, and I will give you rest.*

"'That is a call from Jesus on your life, son. I know your spirit is weary, whether you will admit it to yourself or not. Go to Him; I pray you will.'"

One overpowering difference was made clear as he spoke: he did not only hear this coming from his dad's voice within his memory, but he also heard it from the still, small, but transforming voice of God. He heard it not just in his memory, revealing through bestowed wisdom and revelation that God had been speaking through George to his son; the voice of the Lord was still speaking this to Joash now as he shared his story, continuously calling him to follow Him and seek His kingdom above all else. *Emmanuel, God is with me.* The thought led Joe to become aware of the tangible presence of the Lord heavy on the steps upon which they stood.

"To answer the question you all have beating against your chests, seeking the proper way to ask me: yes, I have come to know Jesus. I believe in God our Creator and my Heavenly Father; I believe Jesus died for me and for all of you. That if you simply call on Him and surrender your lives as I have, as my dad and others have, then you will gain everlasting life and a true relationship with your Creator and savior in that moment. I am brand new to the sonship with my God, yet I already know that I was dead, imprisoned, and lost before I surrendered my life to Him. But now that I have, I will never be any of those ever again. Now I believe I should head into the city and see this thing through. God be with you all."

With not a single further utterance, Joash led his mother, his father, and Spencer to the car to bring them to see through what they had gone to battle for. Human anxiety, worry, and fear were still rolling through his body.

They had not gone from him, but underneath the layer of flesh responses lay a peace and trust newly beginning to form, as though they were an infant or a seed planted. The team of reporters hesitated not to speed off in their own vehicles to chase the story that was about to explode their city with change, newness, and even *faith*. The rest of George's family remained in the doorway waving them off, prior to stepping back inside and hitting their knees in prayer and worship to the One who held it all in His hands. *Hear us, oh God of our righteousness! Make Your path straight before our face. Arise and save us, oh Lord of Hosts, send heaven down to this city, send Your spirit to do Your will. Do not forsake Your hungry and hurting children. Nevertheless not our will but Yours be done!*

* * *

"Hello, Dallas! Welcome to the Truth Is Risen tour! I am so excited to announce this couple who have graciously chosen to lead this tour and who have a story to share that will make it exceedingly difficult for any to doubt that the Truth who is Jesus Christ has risen! Please welcome Joash and Spencer Reis!"

Gliding upon lightless wooden steps toward a far opposite—dare he say blinding—stage, Joash revisited Baker's Peak, as he did while entering every stage he and his wife had been on within the five years of their journey in ministry. A learned, now nearly innate ability birthed amid a frostbitten state in search of

God had allowed a trip to take course along peaks and valleys of thought all while carrying footsteps to proper position ahead of the seats provided to him and Spencer by the kind hosts at every gathering. His fingertips landed, in far less tense repetition, atop his wife's hand, which lay securely around the opposite arm. A previous anxious habit had become a metronome to secure his focus on the Lord leading into prayer. His wife knew well the meaning, causing him to catch a glimpse of her grin in the corner of his eye. Entering his secret place, meeting with Jesus, he began his inward prayer.

Father God in Heaven, I thank You that one day I will ascend into Heaven. All of which I can count on due to my ascension up a mountain where You met me. Same as always, I only ascend any mountain I face by Your will, Your love, Your grace, and Your mercy. I ask as I ascend these steps that You give my wife and me all the above. Speak through us, allow us to not fall into pride, allow us to not seek glory for us, only for You; our purpose is to be vessels through which You can reach more of Your children. Let it be so; let us be so. We submit to You. We resist Satan. It is written and prayed in Jesus's mighty name. Amen.

"Amen," Spencer agreed in a whisper once she became aware his prayer was finished by fingers tapping on her skin. Once again, his short meeting with the Lord had perfect timing as they made their last steps to the center of the stage, turning on their mics.

"Hello, everyone! We're so excited to see you all! For any who do not know us, I am Spencer Reis, and this is my husband, Joash. I am sure most of you have at least heard the name Joe Lar, and if so, you probably know our story. But we're here to tell you a part of our story that the headlines tend to keep out. That story is how we met Jesus and how we came to know without a doubt that *He is alive and risen!*"

Bodies rose from seats; shouts rose from lungs. Spencer and Joash witnessed this often—each encounter brought a raw and real awareness that while to the eye it seemed a simple cheer from a crowd, it was many souls longing for truth, hungering in desperation to be free, to know peace, to know Jesus. They knew this was one of innumerable pieces to their ministry tapestry that the Lord used to fuel and encourage them to continue their trek, regardless of how treacherous a terrain was to be faced. The crowd settled, and along with them, the couple found their seats on stage.

"Greetings, everyone, and thank you for your warm and kind welcome. Though I know your cheers erupted for Jesus far more than us, and we would not have it any other way. There have been moments in this ministry that we have both experienced pride, taking things on as our own, having different complexes that made us think more highly of ourselves than we ought. I believe that is to be expected when you step into ministry. We have flesh, and we have an active enemy who wants nothing more than for us to dive deep into agreement with pride, greed, and sin in and of itself. Each time we fall into a new territory of sin, we are quick to be corrected because we have an even bigger God who is fighting for us to continue to walk with Him and spread His word. However, He will find someone else if we fail; this is His plan, His purpose, and He will carry it out without us. All of that is to say, please check your heart and verify that you are here for Him, not for us. It is you and Jesus alone in this room tonight; let's take a moment to make ourselves aware of such truth." Quiet came swiftly. Prayer began to climb the walls, breach the aisles, and engulf the room.

As His word states, Jesus met them there. *Where two or more are gathered in My name, I will be in their midst.* His word, alive and true, is the only food required to live. Joash recited that scripture before every event, for his longing was to live his life with Jesus, for Jesus. His confirmation regarding the validity of his service in ministry came whenever the tangible presence of the Lord entered the room. The less-than-tangible presence, he learned over time, was the result of copious amounts of meaning. At times it was due to his heart being out of step with the Father's. At times it was to grab his attention for a change in the message to meet a specific need of someone near him. At times it was a test of his faith. He welcomed whatever the Father willed and nothing less, nothing more. The prayers fell silent, and Joash took the mic once more.

"The Truth Is Risen. That title was given to me far before I understood what it would be used for in my life, in our life." His hand reached out to grasp that of his wife. "If any of you knew of me as Joe Lar, you knew Joe Lar was a liar, a cheat, a power-driven, money-hungry crook that lived off grinding others into dust. That fed off the lust of the world. I had no intent to change. Now, skipping over how I made it here for just a moment, you all see sitting before you a man who was a wealthy crook now turned into a minister for Jesus. And I preach from stages often, and I say that Jesus can change your life and bring you victories.

"With that, I urge you to know it may not look like mine. It may not be a ministry our size or larger. It may simply be working your nine-to-five changing just one life around you and walking hand in hand with Jesus yourself. I state that there is no difference in the value of these lives in the kingdom of heaven—Matthew 19:23–26. In all actuality, it is harder for those with large sums of money to make it through Heaven's gates, which is what has me on my knees most nights praying the Father will not allow me to grow in greed or lust for money. Still, you look at me when I share that and say, 'Easy for him to say. This dude never had to go hungry, never had to want for anything. He went from rich to richer.'

"Well, for one, being rich in money means absolutely nothing to God, aside from when we give that money back to Him to bestow onto others. What God seeks in humanity are those who are rich in His spirit, obedience, and humility. You may not even receive that from me or others in my position. And this is something I have been praying on earnestly. How, God, do I get through to others that their ministry, Your work in them, does not revolve around financial success and may not be a stage or a mission trip to Africa? If it is, great, let it be so! But if not, how do I encourage everyone to still seek You even if they view their calling as small?"

Joash stood to his feet and turned slightly toward the stage steps. "I would like to introduce you all to a woman I met through one of our Restoration and Renewal homes. Everyone please give a warm welcome to Kelly!"

A small-framed woman stepped out and made her way to the chair Joash had emptied. Delicate grace was shown in a blaze practically creating visual rays emanating from the sweet soul seated before the crowd. Joash feared bringing her to the stage would seem a circus act, yet it was far from such a thing.

Kelly had come to him without knowing this matter had been on his heart and stated God was calling *her* to encourage others to seek out *whatever* God was calling in *them*. Financial wealth and, more so, fame are such a minuscule part of what the Creator of the world uses to fulfill His purposes. In fact, more often than not, He chooses the lowly to carry forth His plans. The Lord had utilized their ministry to bring souls to Him. To comfort children, raise them, plant them on solid, bountiful grounds. Joash had even had the privilege of leading his old bartender to Jesus. What a story that was. Yet one thorn that caused their ministry to bleed was the masses that saw them only as get-rich-quick scheming liars using the pulpit for financial gain and gatekeeping the "secret" from the rest of the population. It kept hearts bitter and jealous. Joash ached for that to change, making simple the decision to accept Kelly's offer.

The rattle of a gentle hand, a fragile leaf tossed in a chilled whisk of nerves while reaching toward a microphone. Rebuked with a murmured assertion nearly imperceptible to the human ear yet roaring violently in the heavenly realms, halting attackers in an array. Stabilization of a gentle hand, a firm root immovable amid riverbanks. Gripping the mic firmly, she cleared her throat.

"Greetings, everyone. I will begin by stating that this is my first experience being in front of a large crowd; I ask for your patience. Second, it is a good thing my speaking will come directly from the Lord so if there is an issue with it, you all can take it to Him." A ring of giggles in response. "I believe when the Father hears the cry of a heart in need that is to be filled within any ministry He has assigned, He hesitates not to speak a course of action into play. Joash stated earlier that we met through one of the homes. I am not sure how clear the vision of me is from out there, but if you can see clear enough, you would assume we just met last week given the slightly tattered fashion I am sporting."

Laughter arose once more as Kelly pulled a quaint modeling move from her seat, showing off the worn fabric. "I appreciate the joy in the room; the joy of others is something the Lord called me to pour into long ago. As a child I was a bit of an outcast. I recall sitting alone and feeling unseen. That was when the Lord called me to make others seen, and since I have chosen to follow that call, He has confirmed in my heart daily that He sees me.

"I have not always been homeless. I had a normal, dare I say average, life. I had a group of friends who chose to walk around the city and bring care packages to those on the streets. We did, and there is one man whom I will never forget. He would not accept our gift without us allowing him to pray over our ministry and each of us as individuals. We spoke to that man and heard his story of how he ended up on the streets because of PTSD yet how he also chose to stay there to be a rock for the rest of those who were homeless, to give them hope and help them to get out. I knew immediately that was my calling. I gave every one of my belongings away; I gave my home away. I packed a small roller suitcase and moved to a homeless community in an alley."

A plethora of past emotions shimmered across her irises; the remembrance brought grief, joy, pain, thankfulness, sadness, and blessing, a hodgepodge of sensations.

"It has been the hardest, darkest, most painful"—deep breath—"most fulfilling, joyous, bountiful experience I could ever dream of having in this life. If I had to, I would choose it all again. I will not refuse all help when I know that a meal, shelter, warmth, clothing, any gift is of the Lord, from the Lord. I will accept it with open arms. That being said, it is not of the Lord that I remove myself from this life by accepting a whole new life. I am called to live the life of the broken and down while truly being free and restored by my Jesus to connect with them in ways others cannot. To meet them where they are with the heart of someone who understands their pain.

"You see, it takes no money, no fame, no stage, no lights to step into the calling God has for you. You say, 'My job is so small; how can this be what God has for me? How can this be a ministry?' All the while I stand along the sidewalks, completely unseen, no worldly job at all, and the work He's doing through me has moved the same number of mountains in the Kingdom of Heaven as Joash has over here with his calling.

"Now let's not turn on Joash and begin to say that his calling, his purpose, is fake, is less than, is not from the Lord. The Lord utilizes everything in this world for His good, His glory, and His purposes, *if we let Him*. How do we let Him? My suggestion is to study what it means to humbly submit your body and your life to God. That is a good start. And if you think that you're too far from the Lord to be changed and utilized by Him, well, I do believe Mr. Reis is about to share on that. Thank you all; I appreciate your time. But I must get back to where God has planted me. Have a wonderful evening."

A peaceful exit. No cheering lifted. Instead a crowd silenced. Joash stood staring out over the speechless room. He stood in quiet himself, his wife the same, as they simply allowed the Holy Spirit to move over every heart, including their own. An over-abundance of gratitude seeping, pouring, flooding. Thankful for the movement of the Father in this moment. Thankful simply for the Father himself.

* * *

Serene stillness steadied molecules in a hushed room tucked within a bustling hospital. Warmth in a bundle lay atop firm arms. Father held daughter. Teeny lids closed soundly, mild cooing here and there—Joash swayed from side to side, keeping her in comfort as she slept. Mommy lay asleep as well in the bed nearby. It was a lengthy labor, all worth it in the end. "He brought me home and blessed me with my very own flock," Spencer had said moments before dozing off while watching her husband rock her daughter.

As he held this life so loved, he stood peering over the city. The city that held beating hearts and unbelievable stories. Dark, joyous, mundane. Each morning he had to ask for the Father to anoint his mind with oil to understand the reality of the direction his life had begun to travel in. Gideon and Marie had begun to right so many wrongs it caused Joe's head to spin. To grasp the concept that next week he and Spencer had a lunch date with them was seemingly impossible. Then again, the letters they had written George seeking his help and wisdom on coming to know Jesus had been far more of an electrocution. Impossible feats were not only reached but had unbelievably exceeded expectations, exasperating his imagination.

Others had fizzled: folks still hated the Lars and Joe too, which he understood well, choosing to pray for them until they were set free, willing to do whatever it took to help them heal and forgive. Joash still greeted his old foes insecurity, greed, and anger from time to time. Still, each meeting grew shorter, milder. His awareness of how sin separated God's children from His presence, and how God's call on all lives was to choose the path that leads back to Him, a path paved with the blood of Christ; brought sincere revelation of how to love the Father, and how to love all others. How to receive the Father's love, and how to live in love. He had far to go in his trek, yet he had not a single doubt about reaching the peak, there to celebrate for eternity. *Truth is risen, and He raised me too.* Sweet kiss atop an infant's head, sigh of gratitude, set sun. The end of one monumental day, the beginning of a glorious life. *Thank you, Jesus.*

ABOUT THE AUTHOR

Voyage to Yahweh is not just the title of the book, but also the pseudonym of the author. This writer has dedicated their life to providing encouragement and hope through their words. Their writings are deeply influenced by personal experiences and spiritual journeys. *Voyage to Yahweh's* work is characterized by its profound empathy and understanding, making it a beacon for those in need of encouragement. Their book, '*Voyage to Yahweh*', is a testament to their mission, offering readers a journey of self-discovery and resilience.